Tales from Shakespeare

All's Well That Ends Well
&
Measure for Measure

悅讀莎士比亞故事 (8)

終成眷屬。

一報還一報。

Charles and Mary Lamb

CONTENTS

CONTENTS

Principum amicitios!

威廉・莎士比亞（William Shakespeare, 1564-1616）

Shakespeare Centre, Henley St, Stratford-upon-Avon, Warwickshire

莎士比亞簡介

陳敬旻

威廉・莎士比亞（William Shakespeare）出生於英國的史特拉福（Stratford-upon-Avon）。莎士比亞的父親曾任地方議員，母親是地主的女兒。莎士比亞對婦女在廚房或起居室裡勞動的描繪不少，這大概是經由觀察母親所得。他本人也懂得園藝，故作品中的植草種樹表現鮮活。

1571 年，莎士比亞進入公立學校就讀，校內教學多採拉丁文，因此在其作品中到處可見到羅馬詩人奧維德（Ovid）的影子。當時代古典文學的英譯日漸普遍，有學者認為莎士比亞只懂得英語，但這種說法有可議之處。舉例來說，在高登的譯本裡，森林女神只用 Diana 這個名字，而莎士比亞卻在《仲夏夜之夢》一劇中用奧維德原作中的 Titania 一名來稱呼仙后。和莎士比亞有私交的文學家班・強生（Ben Jonson）則曾說，莎翁「懂得一點拉丁文，和一點點希臘文」。

莎士比亞的劇本亦常引用聖經典故，顯示他對新舊約也頗為熟悉。在伊麗莎白女王時期，通俗英語中已有很多聖經詞語。此外，莎士比亞應該很了解當時年輕人所流行的遊戲娛樂，那時也應該有巡迴劇團不時前來史特拉福演出。1575 年，伊麗莎白女王來到郡上時，當地人以化裝遊行、假面戲劇、煙火來款待女王，《仲夏夜之夢》裡就有這種盛會的描繪。

1582 年，莎士比亞與安·海瑟威（Anne Hathaway）結婚，但這場婚姻顯得草率，連莎士比亞的雙親都因不知情而沒有出席婚禮。1586 年，他們在倫敦定居下來。 1586 年的倫敦已是英國首都，年輕人無不想在此大展抱負。史特拉福與倫敦之間的交通頻仍，但對身無長物的人而言，步行仍是最平常的旅行方式。伊麗莎白時期的文學家喜好步行， 1618 年，班·強生就曾在倫敦與愛丁堡之間徒步來回。

莎士比亞初抵倫敦時的史料不充足，因此引發諸多揣測。其中一說為莎士比亞曾在律師處當職員，因為他在劇本與詩歌中經常提及法律術語。但這種説法站不住腳，因為莎士比亞多有訛用，例如他在《威尼斯商人》和《一報還一報》中提到的法律原理及程序，就有諸多錯誤。

事實上，伊麗莎白時期的作家都喜歡引用法律詞彙，這是因為當時的文人和律師時有往來，而且中產階級也常介入訴訟案件，許多法律術語自然為常人所知。莎士比亞樂於援用法律術語，顯示了他對當代生活和風尚的興趣。莎士比亞自抵達倫敦到告老還鄉，心思始終放在戲劇和詩歌上，不太可能接受法律這門專業領域的訓練。

莎士比亞在倫敦的第一份工作是劇場工作。當時常態營業的劇場有兩個：「劇場」（the Theatre）和「帷幕」（the Curtain）。「劇場」的所有人為詹姆士・波比奇（James Burbage），莎士比亞就在此落腳。「劇場」財務狀況不佳，1596 年波比奇過世，把「劇場」交給兩個兒子，其中一個兒子便是著名的悲劇演員理查・波比奇（Richard Burbage）。後來「劇場」因租約問題無法解決，決定將原有的建築物拆除，在泰晤士河對面重建，改名為「環球」（the Globe）。不久，「環球」就展開了戲劇史上空前繁榮的時代。

伊麗莎白時期的戲劇表演只有男演員，所有的女性角色都由男性擔任。演員反串時會戴上面具，效果十足，然而這並不損故事的意境。莎士比亞本身也是一位出色的演員，曾在《皆大歡喜》和《哈姆雷特》中分別扮演忠僕亞當和國王鬼魂這兩個角色。

莎士比亞很留意演員的說白道詞，這點可從哈姆雷特告誡伶人的對話中窺知一二。莎士比亞熟稔劇場的技術與運作，加上他也是劇場股東，故對劇場的營運和組織都甚有研究。不過，他的志業不在演出或劇場管理，而是劇本和詩歌創作。

莎士比亞的戲劇創作始於 1591 年，他當時真正師法的對象是擅長喜劇的約翰‧李利（John Lyly），以及曾寫下轟動一時的悲劇《帖木兒大帝》（*Tamburlaine the Great*）的克里斯多夫‧馬婁（Christopher Marlowe）。莎翁戲劇的特色是兼容並蓄，吸收各家長處，而且他也勤奮多產。一直到 1611 年封筆之前，他每年平均寫出兩部劇作和三卷詩作。莎士比亞慣於在既有的文學作品中尋找材料，又重視大眾喜好，常能讓平淡無奇的作品廣受喜愛。

在當時，劇本都是賣斷給劇場，不能再賣給出版商，因此莎劇的出版先後，並不能反映其創作的時間先後。莎翁作品的先後順序都由後人所推斷，推測的主要依據是作品題材和韻格。他早期的戲劇作品，無論悲劇或喜劇，性質都很單純。隨著創作的手法逐漸成熟，內容愈來愈複雜深刻，悲喜劇熔冶一爐。

自 1591 年席德尼爵士（Sir Philip Sidney）的十四行詩集發表後，十四行詩（sonnets，另譯為商籟）在英國即普遍受到文人的喜愛與仿傚。其中許多作品承續佩脫拉克（Petrarch）的風格，多描寫愛情的酸甜苦樂。莎士比亞的創作一向很能反應當時代的文學風尚，在詩歌體裁鼎盛之時，他也將才華展現在十四行詩上，並將部分作品寫入劇本之中。

莎士比亞的十四行詩主要有兩個主題：婚姻責任和詩歌的不朽。這兩者皆是文藝復興時期詩歌中常見的主題。不少人以為莎士比亞的十四行詩表達了他個人的自省與懺悔，但事實上這些內容有更多是源於他的戲劇天分。

1595 年至 1598 年，莎士比亞陸續寫了《羅密歐與茱麗葉》、《仲夏夜之夢》、《馴悍記》、《威尼斯商人》和若干歷史劇，他的詩歌戲劇也在這段時期受到肯定。當時代的梅爾斯（Francis Meres）就將莎士比亞視為最偉大的文學家，他說：「要是繆思會說英語，一定也會喜歡引用莎士比亞的精彩語藻。」「無論悲劇或喜劇，莎士比亞的表現都是首屈一指。」

闊別故鄉十一年後，莎士比亞於 1596 年返回故居，並在隔年買下名為「新居」（New Place）的房子。那是鎮上第二大的房子，他大幅改建整修，爾後家道日益興盛。莎士比亞有足夠的財力置產並不足以為奇，但他大筆的固定收入主要來自表演，而非劇本創作。當時不乏有成功的演員靠演戲發財，甚至有人將這種現象寫成劇本。

除了表演之外，劇場行政及管理的工作，還有宮廷演出的賞賜，都是他的財源。許多文獻均顯示，莎士比亞是個非常關心財富、地產和社會地位的人，讓許多人感到與他的詩人形象有些扞格不入。

伊麗莎白女王過世後，詹姆士一世（James I）於 1603 年登基，他把莎士比亞所屬的劇團納入保護。莎士比亞此時寫了《第十二夜》和佳評如潮的《哈姆雷特》，成就傲視全英格蘭。但他仍謙恭有禮、溫文爾雅，一如十多前年初抵倫敦的樣子，因此也愈發受到大眾的喜愛。

從這一年起，莎士比亞開始撰寫悲劇《奧賽羅》。他寫悲劇並非是因為精神壓力或生活變故，而是身為一名劇作家，最終目的就是要寫出優秀的悲劇作品。當時他嘗試以詩入劇，在《哈姆雷特》和《一報還一報》中尤其爐火純青。隨後《李爾王》和《馬克白》問世，一直到四年後的《安東尼與克麗奧佩脫拉》，寫作風格登峰造極。

1609 年，倫敦瘟疫猖獗，隔年不見好轉，46 歲的莎士比亞決定告別倫敦，返回史特拉福退隱。 1616 年，莎士比亞和老友德雷頓、班・強生聚會時，可能由於喝得過於盡興，回家後發高燒，一病不起。他將遺囑修改完畢，同年 4 月 23 日，恰巧在他 52 歲的生日當天去世。

七年後，昔日的劇團好友收錄他的劇本做為全集出版，其中有喜劇、歷史劇、悲劇等共 36 個劇本。此書不僅不負莎翁本人所託，也為後人留下珍貴而豐富的文化資源，其中不僅包括美妙動人的詞句，還有各種人物的性格塑造，如高貴、低微、嚴肅或歡樂等性格的著墨。

除了作品，莎士比亞本人也在生前受到讚揚。班‧強生曾說他是個「正人君子，天性開放自由，想像力出奇，擁有大無畏的思想，言詞溫和，蘊含機智。」也有學者以勇敢、敏感、平衡、幽默和身心健康這五種特質來形容莎士比亞，並說他「將無私的愛奉為至上，認為罪惡的根源是恐懼，而非金錢。」

值得一提的是，有人認為這些劇本刻畫入微，具有知性，不可能是未受過大學教育的莎士比亞所寫，因而引發爭議。有人就此推測真正的作者，其中較為人知的有法蘭西斯‧培根（Francis Bacon）和牛津的德維爾公爵（Edward de Vere of Oxford），後者形成了頗具影響力的牛津學派。儘管傳說繪聲繪影，各種假說和研究不斷，但大概已經沒有人會懷疑確有莎士比亞這個人的存在了。

作者簡介：蘭姆姐弟

陳敬旻

姐姐瑪麗（Mary Lamb）生於 1764 年，弟弟查爾斯（Charles Lamb）於 1775 年也在倫敦呱呱落地。因為家境不夠寬裕，瑪麗沒有接受過完整的教育。她從小就做針線活，幫忙持家，照顧母親。查爾斯在學生時代結識了詩人柯立芝（Samuel Taylor Coleridge），兩人成為終生的朋友。查爾斯後來因家中經濟困難而輟學， 1792 年轉而就職於東印度公司（East India House），這是他謀生的終身職業。

查爾斯在二十歲時一度精神崩潰，瑪麗則因為長年工作過量，在 1796 年突然精神病發，持刀攻擊父母，母親不幸傷重身亡。這件人倫悲劇發生後，瑪麗被判為精神異常，送往精神病院。查爾斯為此放棄自己原本期待的婚姻，以便全心照顧姐姐，使她免於在精神病院終老。

十九世紀的英國教育重視莎翁作品，一般的中產階級家庭也希望孩子早點接觸莎劇。1806 年，文學家兼編輯高德溫（William Godwin）邀請查爾斯協助「少年圖書館」的出版計畫，請他將莎翁的劇本改寫為適合兒童閱讀的故事。

查爾斯接受這項工作後就與瑪麗合作，他負責六齣悲劇，瑪麗負責十四齣喜劇並撰寫前言。瑪麗在後來曾描述說，他們兩人「就坐在同一張桌子上改寫，看起來就好像《仲夏夜之夢》裡的荷米雅與海蓮娜一樣。」就這樣，姐弟兩人合力完成了這一系列的莎士比亞故事。《莎士比亞故事集》在 1807 年出版後便大受好評，建立了查爾斯的文學聲響。

查爾斯的寫作風格獨特，筆法樸實，主題豐富。他將自己的一生，包括童年時代、基督教會學校的生活、東印度公司的光陰、與瑪麗相伴的點點滴滴，以及自己的白日夢、鍾愛的書籍和友人等等，都融入在文章裡，作品充滿細膩情感和豐富的想像力。他的軟弱、怪異、魅力、幽默、口吃，在在都使讀者感到親切熟悉，而獨特的筆法與敘事方式，也使他成為英國出色的散文大師。

1823 年，查爾斯和瑪麗領養了一個孤兒愛瑪。兩年後，查爾斯自東印度公司退休，獲得豐厚的退休金。查爾斯的健康情形和瑪麗的精神狀況卻每況愈下。 1833 年，愛瑪嫁給出版商後，又只剩下姐弟兩人。 1834 年 7 月，由於幼年時代的好友柯立芝去世，查爾斯的精神一蹶不振，沉湎酒精。此年秋天，查爾斯在散步時不慎跌倒，傷及顏面，後來傷口竟惡化至不可收拾的地步，而於年底過世。

查爾斯善與人交，他和同時期的許多文人都保持良好情誼，又因他一生對姐姐的照顧不餘遺力，所以也廣受敬佩。查爾斯和瑪麗兩人都終生未婚，查爾斯曾在一篇伊利亞小品中，將他們的狀況形容為「雙重單身」（double singleness）。查爾斯去世後，瑪麗的心理狀態雖然漸趨惡化，但仍繼續活了十三年之久。

All's Well That Ends Well

終 成 眷 屬

導讀

陳敬旻

女性拯救者

在民間故事裡，常可見出身低微卻擁有無比勇氣、智慧或能力的青年，在圓滿完成如屠龍、解謎、治病等最艱難的任務後，國王或公爵就會把美麗的公主許配給他。《終成眷屬》的內容與此類似，只是智勇雙全的主角變成了女性，最終的獎賞則變成了男性。

這種性別替換並非是莎士比亞自創的想法，而是源自於潘特（William Painter）於 1566-67 年間出版（1575 年修訂）的英譯故事集《愉悅的殿堂》（*The Palace of Pleasure*）。此書收錄了薄伽丘（Boccaccio）《十日談》（*Decameron*）裡第三天的第九個故事，描述女主人翁治癒國王，並兩度贏得夫婿而終成眷屬的故事。

在本劇裡，女主角海倫娜（Helena）以神奇藥方治好國王的痼疾，從而得以與暗戀已久的心上人貝特漢（Bertram）成婚。但貝特漢不滿這樁婚姻，忿而離開家園，遠赴義大利從軍，並在當地愛上一位名為黛安娜（Diana）的女子。

遭到遺棄的海倫娜傷心出走，她途經義大利時，得知丈夫的消息，便心生一計，在貝特漢即將返回法國的前一晚，假扮成黛安娜，與貝特漢共度一宵，並交換戒指作為定情物。海倫娜取得貝特漢手中的戒指後，貝特漢只得履行自己的承諾，永遠愛著海倫娜。海倫娜二度智取貝特漢，如願成為伯爵夫人，而國王也賜給黛安娜一名貴族丈夫。

此劇其實已不屬於喜劇範疇，因為在喜劇中，主要人物幾乎都要經過一番磨難後，才能獲得圓滿的結局。反觀《終成眷屬》，海倫娜歷經的各種悲喜起伏，都不像喜劇般確定，常常與讀者的預期產生落差。例如，國王病入膏肓，御醫束手無策，而毫無經驗的海倫娜卻能憑著一帖神奇藥方讓國王康復。又例如，當貝特漢奉命與海倫娜成親，看似已經成功的計畫，卻又因貝特漢的頑固高傲讓海倫娜失望。

在一切彷彿陷入絕境之時，海倫娜竟然又巧獲貝特漢的消息，並利用一個難以令人信服的「床上把戲」（bed trick），完成另一項不可能的任務。最後，當海倫娜終於讓丈夫回頭後，國王也在此時答應讓黛安娜在群臣中挑選丈夫。

「陰鬱喜劇」和「問題劇」

整個故事看似圓滿地以喜劇收場，但讀者的預期經過三番兩次的落差後，卻不相信這是真正的結局，反而會猜想黛安娜自己挑選的婚姻，將可能會步上海倫娜與貝特漢的後塵，同樣的故事將重新上演。也因此，學者及評論家普遍認為《終成眷屬》並非喜劇，而是「陰鬱喜劇」（dark comedy）或「問題劇」（problem play）。

KING. Now, fair one, does your business follow us?

HELENA. Ay, my good lord.

最早提出這個概念的是 F. S. Boas，他在 1896 年將此劇視為「問題劇」。他解釋，戲中營造的「不是全然的歡愉也非全然的痛苦，但觀眾卻為之振奮、著迷、困惑」，而劇中的問題到最後也獲得令人滿意的結果。或許這只是指表面上令人滿意的結果，至於其後將引發的危機或變數，隨著劇作家停筆就嘎然而止了。

本劇並沒有公開演出的紀錄，劇本在當時也沒有印行，而是在莎士比亞死後七年才出版的第一對開本（the First Folio）裡首次面世，因此產生了此劇寫作年代的考證與爭論。許多人都將《終成眷屬》與《一報還一報》（Measure for Measure）來相提並論，因為這兩齣戲都是寶斯眼中的問題劇，而且由《終成眷屬》的風格及語言特徵來推斷，此劇約完成於 1602-3 年，正好就在《一報還一報》（1604 年）之前。

本劇的韻文濃縮、簡略、抽象、模糊，也與《一報還一報》的語法相近，更有甚者，兩劇在終了時都是利用「床上把戲」，達到童話故事般的和諧結局，卻在現實世界裡顯得格格不入。

持反對意見的人則認為，類似的劇情在莎劇作中出現，並不能證明寫作年代相近，例如「船難」事件就在他早期的《連環錯》（The Comedy of Errors）、中期的《第十二夜》（Twelfth Night）、晚期的《暴風雨》（The Tempest）裡都出現過；而《終成眷屬》的靈魂人物海倫娜為兼具膽識、智慧和美貌的女性，又與《威尼斯商人》（The Merchant of Venice）的波兒榭（Portia）、《皆大歡喜》（As You Like It）的羅莎琳（Rosalind）、《第十二夜》的菲兒拉（Viola）很像，而這些劇本都是在 1596 至 1600 年間寫成的。

儘管如此，多數學者仍將《終成眷屬》列為十七世紀的作品。因為莎士比亞在十七世紀初時，將主要的心思都放在創作悲劇上，《哈姆雷特》（*Hamlet*）、《奧賽羅》（*Othello*）、《李爾王》（*King Lear*）、《馬克白》（*Macbeth*）都是這個階段的作品，而問題劇的主旨、調性及語言都較為接近悲劇，而不似 1590 年代後期的喜劇。

父母與女性的角色

自羅馬時期的希臘喜劇作家米南德（Menander）開始（約西元前四世紀），年輕男女會為了愛情竭盡全力跨越階級和門第之見，而老一輩的父母、伯叔等則是千篇一律地站在反對的另一邊。

莎士比亞早期的作品如《仲夏夜之夢》及《羅密歐與茱麗葉》（*Romeo and Juliet*）也遵循著這種模式，但到了《終成眷屬》，他似乎想打破這個不成文的安排，使劇中的長者展現慈愛與包容之心：國王不嫌棄海倫娜的出身，將貝特漢許配給她；老臣拉福支持她；伯爵夫人則滿心歡喜地接受她為媳婦。反之，年輕一輩的貝特漢卻顯得自視過高。

本劇的另一個特點是性別觀，其和傳統的性別角色限定有所不同。最明顯的例子是海倫娜猛追自己心儀的男子。此外，在民間故事裡，男選女之後，女方的意願無人聞問，而在這個女選男故事裡，男方的意願卻顯得很重要。

十七世紀初的監護權和對於性操守的法律規範，在英國仍受爭議。反對者認為，監護人常不考慮受監護人的個人意願，便妄作決定。贊成的人則表示，監護人有必要幫助受監護人免於外來的引誘，以免喪失地位、財產或繼承權。

監護權和性操守這兩項議題一經結合，就產生了另一項議題：「性行為究竟是屬於個人事件，還是公眾事件？」以《終成眷屬》為例，莎士比亞似乎贊成由年長者或法律條文來匡正年輕人的性觀念和性行為，引其走上婚姻的正途，例如伯爵夫人、拉福和國王都代表這一角色。

莎士比亞撰寫本劇時，他的兩個女兒都已到了適婚年齡，因此家庭成員對婚姻的影響力，在他的劇作裡也就愈形彰顯。從這個角度來看，本劇還標誌著莎士比亞將人物重心逐漸轉移到年長世代的過渡期。

這種轉移也獲得蕭伯納的讚許，他認為，伯爵夫人是西方戲劇史上描寫得最完美的老婦人，而海倫娜與貝特漢之間的情緒反應也極為逼真。無怪乎若干學者不將海倫娜克服萬難的英雌事蹟視為《終成眷屬》的主旨，而是把愛情與婚姻當作此劇的核心。

人物表

Bertram	貝特漢	盧西昂伯爵貝，恃才傲物
Helena	海倫娜	名醫之女,愛慕貝特漢
the countess	伯爵夫人	貝特漢之母
King of France	法王	為海倫娜賜婚,許配給貝特漢
Lafeu	拉福	法國宮廷的老臣
the widow	寡婦	一個殷勤好客的寡婦
Diana	黛安娜	寡婦之女,為貝特漢所著迷

All's Well That Ends Well

🎧 Bertram, Count of Rousillon, had newly come to that title and estate, by the death of his father. The King of France loved the father of Bertram, and when he heard of his death, he sent for his son to come immediately to his royal court in Paris, intending, for the friendship he bore the late count, to grace young Bertram with his especial favor and protection.

Bertram was living with his mother, the widowed countess, when Lafeu, an old lord of the French court; came to conduct him to the king. The King of France was an absolute monarch[1] and the invitation to court was in the form of a royal mandate[2], or positive command, which no subject, of what high dignity soever, might disobey; therefore though the countess, in parting with this dear son, seemed a second time to bury her husband, whose loss she had so lately mourned, yet she dared not to keep him a single day, but gave instant orders for his departure.

1 monarch ['mɑːnərk] (n.) 君主（國王、女王、皇帝、女皇）
2 mandate ['mændeɪt] (n.) 命令；訓令

Lafeu, who came to fetch him, tried to comfort the countess for the loss of her late lord, and her son's sudden absence; and he said, in a courtier's[3] flattering manner, that the king was so kind a prince, she would find in his majesty a husband, and that he would be a father to her son; meaning only, that the good king would befriend the fortunes of Bertram.

Lafeu told the countess that the king had fallen into a sad malady[4], which was pronounced by his physicians to be incurable. The lady expressed great sorrow on hearing this account of the king's ill health, and said, she wished the father of Helena (a young gentlewoman who was present in attendance upon her) were living, for that she doubted not he could have cured his majesty of his disease.

---

3 courtier ['kɔːrtɪr] (n.) 朝臣（朝廷中的侍臣）
4 malady ['mælədi] (n.) 疾病

🎧 3   And she told Lafeu something of the history of Helena, saying she was the only daughter of the famous physician Gerard de Narbon, and that he had recommended his daughter to her care when he was dying, so that since his death she had taken Helena under her protection; then the countess praised the virtuous disposition[5] and excellent qualities of Helena, saying she inherited these virtues from her worthy father.

While she was speaking, Helena wept in sad and mournful silence, which made the countess gently reprove[6] her for too much grieving for her father's death.

Bertram now bade his mother farewell. The countess parted with this dear son with tears and many blessings, and commended[7] him to the care of Lafeu, saying, "Good my lord, advise him, for he is an unseasoned[8] courtier."

---

5 disposition [ˌdɪspəˈzɪʃən] (n.) 性情；氣質
6 reprove [rɪˈpruːv] (v.) 責罵；譴責
7 commend [kəˈmend] (v.) 將某事物託付給……；託……保管
8 unseasoned [ʌnˈsiːzənd] (a.)（指木材）未長成的；（指食物）沒有調味的

🎧 Bertram's last words were spoken to Helena, but they were words of mere civility, wishing her happiness; and he concluded his short farewell to her with saying, "Be comfortable to my mother, your mistress, and make much of her."

Helena had long loved Bertram, and when she wept in sad and mournful silence, the tears she shed were not for Gerard de Narbon. Helena loved her father, but in the present feeling of a deeper love, the object of which she was about to lose, she had forgotten the very form and features of her dead father, her imagination presenting no image to her mind but Bertram's.

Helena had long loved Bertram, yet she always remembered that he was the Count of Rousillon, descended[9] from the most ancient family in France; she was of humble birth; her parents were of no note at all; his ancestors all noble. And therefore she looked up to the high-born Bertram as to her master and to her dear lord, and dared not form any wish but to live his servant, and so living to die his vassal[10].

9 descend [dɪ'send] (v.) （指財產、氣質、權利等）遺傳；傳代
10 vassal ['væsəl] (n.) （喻）謙恭的從屬者；下屬

Act. 1   Scene. 3

HELENA.   Then, I confess,
Here on my knee, before high heaven and you,
That before you, and next unto high heaven,
I love your son.

🎧(5)   So great the distance seemed to her between his height of dignity and her lowly fortunes, that she would say, "It were all one that I should love a bright particular star, and think to wed it, Bertram is so far above me."

Bertram's absence filled her eyes with tears and her heart with sorrow; for though she loved without hope, yet it was a pretty comfort to her to see him every hour, and Helena would sit and look upon his dark eye, his arched brow, and the curls of his fine hair, till she seemed to draw his portrait on the tablet of her heart, that heart too capable of retaining the memory of every line in the features of that loved face.

Gerard de Narbon, when he died, left her no other portion than some prescriptions[11] of rare and well-proved virtue, which by deep study and long experience in medicine he had collected as sovereign[12] and almost infallible[13] remedies.

---

11 prescription [prɪˈskrɪpʃən] (n.) 所規定之事物尤指醫生開的處
方；處方上的藥
12 sovereign [ˈsɑːvrən] (a.) （指權力）至高無上的
13 infallible [ɪnˈfælɪbəl] (a.) 絕對可靠的

Among the rest, there was one set down as an approved medicine for the disease under which Lafeu said the king at that time languished[14]: and when Helena heard of the king's complaint, she, who till now had been so humble and so hopeless, formed an ambitious project in her mind to go herself to Paris, and undertake the cure of the king.

But though Helena was the possessor of this choice prescription, it was unlikely, as the king as well as his physicians was of opinion that his disease was incurable, that they would give credit to a poor unlearned virgin, if she should offer to perform a cure. The firm hopes that Helena had of succeeding, if she might be permitted to make the trial, seemed more than even her father's skill warranted, though he was the most famous physician of his time; for she felt a strong faith that this good medicine was sanctified[15] by all the luckiest stars in heaven to be the legacy[16] that should advance her fortune, even to the high dignity of being Count Rousillon's wife.

14 languished ['læŋgwɪʃt] (a.) 衰弱無力的；因渴望而煩惱的
15 sanctify ['sæŋktɪfaɪ] (v.) 使神聖；尊崇
16 legacy ['legəsi] (n.) 遺產；遺贈物

Bertram had not been long gone, when the countess was informed by her steward, that he had overheard Helena talking to herself, and that he understood from some words she uttered, she was in love with Bertram, and thought of following him to Paris. The countess dismissed the steward with thanks, and desired him to tell Helena she wished to speak with her.

What she had just heard of Helena brought the remembrance of days long past into the mind of the countess; those days probably when her love for Bertram's father first began; and she said to herself, "Even so it was with me when I was young. Love is a thorn that belongs to the rose of youth; for in the season of youth, if ever we are nature's children, these faults are ours, though then we think not they are faults."

While the countess was thus meditating on the loving errors of her own youth, Helena entered.

🎧⑧ And she said to her, "Helena, you know I am a mother to you."

Helena replied, "You are my honorable mistress."

"You are my daughter," said the countess again: "I say I am your mother. Why do you start and look pale at my words?"

With looks of alarm and confused thoughts, fearing the countess suspected her love, Helena still replied, "Pardon me, madam, you are not my mother; the Count Rousillon cannot be my brother, nor I your daughter."

"Yet, Helena," said the countess, "you might be my daughter-in-law; and I am afraid that is what you mean to be, the words mother and daughter so disturb you. Helena, do you love my son?"

"Good madam, pardon me," said the affrighted Helena.

Again the countess repeated her question, "Do you love my son?"

"Do not you love him, madam?" said Helena.

The countess replied, "Give me not this evasive[17] answer, Helena. Come, come, disclose the state of your affections, for your love has to the full appeared."

---

17 evasive [ɪˈveɪsɪv] (a.) 躲避的；逃避的；避免的

Countess and Helena

Helena on her knees now owned her love, and with shame and terror implored[18] the pardon of her noble mistress; and with words expressive of the sense she had of the inequality between their fortunes, she protested Bertram did not know she loved him, comparing her humble unaspiring[19] love to a poor Indian, who adores the sun that looks upon his worshiper, but knows of him no more.

The countess asked Helena if she had not lately an intent to go to Paris. Helena owned the design she had formed in her mind, when she heard Lafeu speak of the king's illness.

"This was your motive for wishing to go to Paris," said the countess. "Was it? Speak truly."

Helena honestly answered, "My lord your son made me to think of this; else Paris, and the medicine, and the king, had from the conversation of my thoughts been absent then."

The countess heard the whole of this confession without saying a word either of approval or of blame, but she strictly questioned Helena as to the probability of the medicine being useful to the king.

---

18 implore [ɪmˈplɔːr] (v.) 懇求；哀求
19 unaspiring [ˌʌnəˈspaɪərɪŋ] (a.) 追求不到的

🎧10 She found that it was the most prized by Gerard de Narbon of all he possessed, and that he had given it to his daughter on his deathbed; and remembering the solemn promise she had made at that awful hour in regard to this young maid, whose destiny and the life of the king himself, seemed to depend on the execution of a project (which though conceived[20] by the fond suggestions of a loving maiden's thoughts, the countess knew not but it might be the unseen workings of Providence[21] to bring to pass the recovery of the king, and to lay the foundation of the future fortunes of Gerard de Narbon's daughter), free leave she gave to Helena to pursue her own way, and generously furnished her with ample[22] means and suitable attendants and Helena set out for Paris with the blessings of the countess, and her kindest wishes for her success.

20 conceive [kən'siːv] (v.) 構思；計畫
21 Providence ['prɑːvɪdəns] (n.)〔作大寫〕上帝；天佑
22 ample ['æmpəl] (a.) 充足的；豐富的

🎧 Helena arrived at Paris, and by the assistance of her friend the old Lord Lafeu, she obtained an audience of the king. She had still many difficulties to encounter, for the king was not easily prevailed[23] on to try the medicine offered him by this fair young doctor. But she told him she was Gerard de Narbon's daughter (with whose fame the king was well acquainted) and she offered the precious medicine as the darling treasure which contained the essence of all her father's long experience and skill, and she boldly engaged to forfeit[24] her life, if it failed to restore his majesty to perfect health in the space of two days.

The king at length consented to try it, and in two days' time Helena was to lose her life if the king did not recover; but if she succeeded, he promised to give her the choice of any man throughout all France (the princes only excepted) whom she could like for a husband; the choice of a husband being the fee Helena demanded if she cured the king of his disease.

---

23 prevail [prɪ'veɪl] (v.) 勸導
24 forfeit ['fɔːrfɪt] (v.) 作為懲罰或結果，或由於規則等而喪失；被沒收

KING.   Know'st thou not, Bertram,
            What she has done for me?
BERTRAM. Yes, my good lord; but never hope to know why
            I should marry her.

🎧12 Helena did not deceive herself in the hope she conceived of the efficacy[25] of her father's medicine. Before two days were at an end, the king was restored to perfect health, and he assembled all the young noblemen of his court together, in order to confer[26] the promised reward of a husband upon his fair physician; and he desired Helena to look round on this youthful parcel of noble bachelors, and choose her husband.

Helena was not slow to make her choice, for among these young lords she saw the Count Rousillon, and turning to Bertram, she said, "This is the man. I dare not say, my lord I take you, but I give me and my service ever whilst[27] I live into your guiding power."

"Why, then," said the king, "young Bertram, take her; she is your wife."

Bertram did not hesitate to declare his dislike to this present of the king's of the self-offered Helena, who, he said, was a poor physician's daughter, bred at his father's charge, and now living a dependent on his mother's bounty[28].

25 efficacy ['efɪkəsi] (n.)（不用於指人）有效；效能
26 confer [kən'fɜːr] (v.) 授與（學位、頭銜、恩惠）
27 whilst [waɪlst] (conj.) 當……的時候；在……之時；和……同時
28 bounty ['baʊnti] (n.)〔正式〕慷慨；好施

🎧 13 Helena heard him speak these words of rejection and of scorn[29], and she said to the king, "That you are well, my lord, I am glad. Let the rest go."

But the king would not suffer his royal command to be so slighted; for the power of bestowing[30] their nobles in marriage was one of the many privileges of the kings of France; and that same day Bertram was married to Helena, a forced and uneasy marriage to Bertram, and of no promising hope to the poor lady, who, though she gained the noble husband she had hazarded[31] her life to obtain, seemed to have won but a splendid blank, her husband's love not being a gift in the power of the King of France to bestow.

Helena was no sooner married, than she was desired by Bertram to apply to the king for him for leave of absence from court; and when she brought him the king's permission for his departure, Bertram told her that he was not prepared for this sudden marriage, it had much unsettled him, and therefore she must not wonder at the course he should pursue.

If Helena wondered not, she grieved when she found it was his intention to leave her.

---

29 scorn [skɔːrn] (n.) 輕蔑；蔑視
30 bestow [bɪˈstoʊ] (v.) 給與；授與；賜贈
31 hazard [ˈhæzərd] (v.) 冒⋯⋯之險；遭受危險

King and Helena

He ordered her to go home to his mother. When Helena heard this unkind command, she replied, "Sir, I can nothing say to this, but that I am your most obedient servant, and shall ever with true observance[32] seek to eke[33] out that desert, wherein my homely stars have failed to equal my great fortunes."

But this humble speech of Helena's did not at all move the haughty[34] Bertram to pity his gentle wife, and he parted from her without even the common civility of a kind farewell.

Back to the countess then Helena returned. She had accomplished the purport[35] of her journey, she had preserved the life of the king, and she had wedded her heart's dear lord, the Count Rousillon; but she returned back a dejected lady to her noble mother-in-law, and as soon as she entered the house she received a letter from Bertram which almost broke her heart.

---

32 observance [əb'zɜːrvəns] (n.) （法律、習俗、節日等的）遵守；
　　　奉行
33 eke [iːk] (v.) 補足；力求維持（生活）
34 haughty ['hɑːti] (a.) 傲慢的；驕傲的
35 purport [pɜːr'pɔːrt] (n.)〔正式〕主旨；意義；一個人的行動之
　　可能解釋

BERTRAM. This to my mother.

Act. 2 Scene. 5

The good countess received her with a cordial[36] welcome, as if she had been her son's own choice, and a lady of a high degree, and she spoke kind words to comfort her for the unkind neglect of Bertram in sending his wife home on her bridal day alone.

Bertram and Helena

But this gracious reception failed to cheer the sad mind of Helena, and she said, "Madam, my lord is gone, forever gone."

She then read these words out of Bertram's letter:

When you can get the ring from my finger,
which never shall come off, then call me husband,
but in such a Then I write a Never.

---

36 cordial [ˈkɔːrdʒəl] (a.) (在情感或行為上)熱誠;懇摯的

🎧16 "This is a dreadful sentence!" said Helena.

The countess begged her to have patience, and said, now Bertram was gone, she should be her child, and that she deserved a lord that twenty such rude boys as Bertram might tend upon, and hourly call her mistress. But in vain by respectful condescension[37] and kind flattery this matchless mother tried to soothe[38] the sorrows of her daughter-in-law.

Helena still kept her eyes fixed upon the letter, and cried out in an agony[39] of grief,

Till I have no wife,
I have nothing in France.

The countess asked her if she found those words in the letter.

"Yes, madam," was all poor Helena could answer.

---

37 condescension [ˌkɑːndɪˈsenʃən] (n.) 屈尊；俯就
38 soothe [suːð] (v.) （使痛苦或疼痛）緩和或減輕
39 agony [ˈæɡəni] (n.) （精神或肉體上的）極大的痛苦

🎧 **17** The next morning Helena was missing. She left a letter to be delivered to the countess after she was gone, to acquaint her with the reason of her sudden absence: in this letter she informed her that she was so much grieved at having driven Bertram from his native country and his home, that to atone[40] for her offense, she had undertaken a pilgrimage[41] to the shrine of St. Jaques le Grand, and concluded with requesting the countess to inform her son that the wife he so hated had left his house forever.

Bertram, when he left Paris, went to Florence, and there became an officer in the Duke of Florence's army, and after a successful war, in which he distinguished himself by many brave actions, Bertram received letters from his mother, containing the acceptable tidings[42] that Helena would no more disturb him.

And he was preparing to return home, when Helena herself, clad[43] in her pilgrim's weeds, arrived at the city of Florence.

---

40 atone [əˈtoʊn] (v.) 彌補；補償；贖罪
41 pilgrimage [ˈpɪlgrɪmɪdʒ] (n.) 朝聖者的旅程
42 tidings [ˈtaɪdɪŋz] (n.)〔古〕消息；音信
43 clad [klæd] (v.) clothe 的舊式過去分詞

🎧 (18)   Florence was a city through which the pilgrims used to pass on their way to St. Jaques le Grand; and when Helena arrived at this city, she heard that a hospitable widow dwelt there, who used to receive into her house the female pilgrims that were going to visit the shrine of that saint, giving them lodging and kind entertainment. To this good lady, therefore, Helena went, and the widow gave her a courteous welcome, and invited her to see whatever was curious in that famous city, and told her that if she would like to see the duke's army, she would take her where she might have a full view of it.

"And you will see a countryman of yours," said the widow; "his name is Count Rousillon, who has done worthy service in the duke's wars."

Helena wanted no second invitation, when she found Bertram was to make part of the show. She accompanied her hostess; and a sad and mournful pleasure it was to her to look once more upon her dear husband's face.

"Is he not a handsome man?" said the widow.

"I like him well," replied Helena, with great truth.

Helena

🎧 19 All the way they walked, the talkative widow's discourse was all of Bertram: she told Helena the story of Bertram's marriage, and how he had deserted the poor lady his wife, and entered into the duke's army to avoid living with her.

To this account of her own misfortunes Helena patiently listened, and when it was ended, the history of Bertram was not yet done, for then the widow began another tale, every word of which sank deep into the mind of Helena; for the story she now told was of Bertram's love for her daughter.

Though Bertram did not like the marriage forced on him by the king, it seems he was not insensible to love, for since he had been stationed[44] with the army at Florence, he had fallen in love with Diana, a fair young gentlewoman, the daughter of this widow who was Helena's hostess; and every night, with music of all sorts, and songs composed in praise of Diana's beauty, he would come under her window, and solicit[45] her love; and all his suit to her was, that she would permit him to visit her by stealth after the family were retired to rest.

---

44 station ['steɪʃən] (v.) 安置；配置
45 solicit [sə'lɪsɪt] (v.) 懇求；乞求

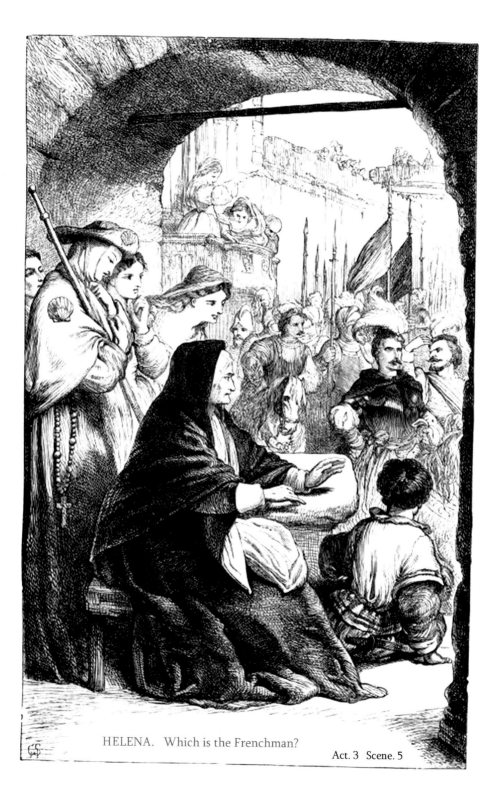

HELENA.   Which is the Frenchman?

Act. 3   Scene. 5

🎧20 But Diana would by no means be persuaded to grant this improper request, nor give any encouragement to his suit, knowing him to be a married man; for Diana had been brought up under the counsels[46] of a prudent mother, who, though she was now in reduced circumstances, was well born, and descended from the noble family of the Capulets.

All this the good lady related to Helena, highly praising the virtuous principles of her discreet daughter, which she said were entirely owing to the excellent education and good advice she had given her; and she further said, that Bertram had been particularly importunate[47] with Diana to admit him to the visit he so much desired that night, because he was going to leave Florence early the next morning.

Though it grieved Helena to hear of Bertram's love for the widow's daughter, yet from this story the ardent[48] mind of Helena conceived a project (nothing discouraged at the ill success of her former one) to recover her truant[49] lord.

---

46 counsel ['kaʊnsəl] (n.)（用不定冠詞連用或用複數，但不與數字連用）勸告；忠告
47 importunate [ɪm'pɔːrtʃʊnɪt] (a.)（指事務等）急切的
48 ardent ['ɑːrdənt] (a.) 熱心的；熱情的
49 truant ['truːənt] (a.)〔形容用法〕（指人思想、行為等）怠惰的；規避（責任）的

⌢21 She disclosed to the widow that she was Helena, the deserted wife of Bertram and requested that her kind hostess and her daughter would suffer this visit from Bertram to take place, and allow her to pass herself upon Bertram for Diana; telling them, her chief motive for desiring to have this secret meeting with her husband, was to get a ring from him, which he had said, if ever she was in possession of he would acknowledge her as his wife.

The widow and her daughter promised to assist her in this affair, partly moved by pity for this unhappy forsaken wife, and partly won over to her interest by the promises of reward which Helena made them, giving them a purse of money in earnest of her future favor.

In the course of that day Helena caused information to be sent to Bertram that she was dead; hoping that when he thought himself free to make a second choice by the news of her death, he would offer marriage to her in her feigned [50] character of Diana. And if she could obtain the ring and this promise too, she doubted not she should make some future good come of it.

---

50 feigned [feɪnd] (a.) 假裝的

In the evening, after it was dark, Bertram was admitted into Diana's chamber, and Helena was there ready to receive him.

The flattering compliments and love discourse he addressed to Helena were precious sounds to her, though she knew they were meant for Diana; and Bertram was so well pleased with her, that he made her a solemn promise to be her husband, and to love her forever; which she hoped would be prophetic of a real affection, when he should know it was his own wife, the despised Helena, whose conversation had so delighted him.

Bertram never knew how sensible a lady Helena was, else perhaps he would not have been so regardless of her; and seeing her every day, he had entirely overlooked her beauty; a face we are accustomed to see constantly, losing the effect which is caused by the first sight either of beauty or of plainness; and of her understanding it was impossible he should judge, because she felt such reverence, mixed with her love for him, that she was always silent in his presence.

BERTRAM. Here, take my ring:
My house, mine honour, yea, my life, be thine,
And I'll be bid by thee.

Act. 4 Scene. 2

Act. 4 Scene. 2

 But now that her future fate, and the happy ending of all her love-projects, seemed to depend on her leaving a favorable impression on the mind of Bertram from this night's interview, she exerted[51] all her wit to please him; and the simple graces of her lively conversation and the endearing sweetness of her manners so charmed Bertram, that he vowed she should be his wife.

51 exert [ɪgˈzɜːrt] (v.) 發揮；運用

⏻24 Helena begged the ring from off his finger as a token[52] of his regard, and he gave it to her; and in return for this ring, which it was of such importance to her to possess, she gave him another ring, which was one the king had made her a present of.

Before it was light in the morning, she sent Bertram away; and he immediately set out on his journey toward his mother's house.

Helena prevailed on the widow and Diana to accompany her to Paris, their further assistance being necessary to the full accomplishment of the plan she had formed. When they arrived there, they found the king was gone upon a visit to the Countess of Rousillon, and Helena followed the king with all the speed she could make.

The king was still in perfect health, and his gratitude to her who had been the means of his recovery was so lively in his mind, that the moment he saw the Countess of Rousillon, he began to talk of Helena, calling her a precious jewel that was lost by the folly of her son; but seeing the subject distressed the countess, who sincerely lamented[53] the death of Helena, he said, "My good lady, I have forgiven and forgotten all."

---

52 token ['toukən] (n.) 證據；象徵；記號
53 lament [lə'ment] (v.) 悲傷；惋惜

Bertram
and
Diana

But the good-natured old Lafeu, who was present, and could not bear that the memory of his favorite Helena should be so lightly passed over, said, "This I must say, the young lord did great offense to his majesty, his mother, and his lady; but to himself he did the greatest wrong of all, for he has lost a wife whose beauty astonished all eyes, whose words took all ears captive[54], whose deep perfection made all hearts wish to serve her."

The king said, "Praising what is lost makes the remembrance dear. Well— call him hither;" meaning Bertram, who now presented himself before the king: and on his expressing deep sorrow for the injuries he had done to Helena, the king, for his dead father's and his admirable mother's sake, pardoned him and restored him once more to his favor.

---

54 captive ['kæptɪv] (n.) 俘虜；被俘虜的（人）；被捕獲的（動物）

KING.   Now, pray you, let me see it; for mine eye,   Act. 5   Scene. 3
          While I was speaking, oft was fasten'd to't.

26   But the gracious countenance of the king was soon
changed toward him, for he perceived that Bertram
wore the very ring upon his finger which he had given
to Helena: and he well remembered that Helena had
called all the saints in heaven to witness she would
never part with that ring, unless she sent it to the
king himself upon some great disaster befalling her;
and Bertram, on the king's questioning him how he
came by the ring, told an improbable story of a lady
throwing it to him out of a window, and denied ever
having seen Helena since the day of their marriage.

🎧⟨27⟩ The king, knowing Bertram's dislike to his wife, feared he had destroyed her: and he ordered his guards to seize Bertram, saying, "I am wrapt in dismal[55] thinking, for I fear the life of Helena was foully snatched."

At this moment Diana and her mother entered, and presented a petition[56] to the king, wherein they begged his majesty to exert his royal power to compel[57] Bertram to marry Diana, he having made her a solemn promise of marriage. Bertram, fearing the king's anger, denied he had made any such promise; and then Diana produced the ring (which Helena had put into her hands) to confirm the truth of her words; and she said that she had given Bertram the ring he then wore, in exchange for that, at the time he vowed to marry her.

On hearing this the king ordered the guards to seize her also; and her account of the ring differing from Bertram's, the king's suspicions were confirmed: and he said, if they did not confess how they came by this ring of Helena's, they should be both put to death.

---

55 dismal [ˈdɪzməl] (a.) 憂愁的
56 petition [pɪˈtɪʃən] (n.) （尤指）請願書；陳情書
57 compel [kəmˈpel] (v.) 強迫；迫使

KING.   Come hither, count; do you know these women?
BERTRAM. My lord, I neither can nor will deny
           But that I know them: do they charge me further?

28 Diana requested her mother might be permitted to fetch the jeweler of whom she bought the ring, which being granted, the widow went out, and presently returned, leading in Helena herself.

The good countess, who in silent grief had beheld her son's danger, and had even dreaded that the suspicion of his having destroyed his wife might possibly be true, finding her dear Helena, whom she loved with even a maternal[58] affection, was still living, felt a delight she was hardly able to support; and the king, scarce believing for joy that it was Helena, said, "Is this indeed the wife of Bertram that I see?"

Helena, feeling herself yet an unacknowledged wife, replied, "No, my good lord, it is but the shadow of a wife you see, the name and not the thing."

Bertram cried out, "Both, both! Oh pardon!"

"O my lord," said Helena, "when I personated[59] this fair maid, I found you wondrous kind; and look, here is your letter!" reading to him in a joyful tone those words which she had once repeated so sorrowfully, "*When from my finger you can get this ring*— This is done; it was to me you gave the ring. Will you be mine, now you are doubly won?"

---

58 maternal [məˈtɜːrnl] (a.) 母親的；似母親的
59 personate [ˈpɜːrsəneɪt] (v.) 扮演；飾演（戲中某一角色）

Bertram replied, "If you can make it plain that you were the lady I talked with that night, I will love you dearly ever, ever dearly."

This was no difficult task, for the widow and Diana came with Helena to prove this fact; and the king was so well pleased with Diana for the friendly assistance she had rendered[60] the dear lady he so truly valued for the service she had done him, that he promised her also a noble husband: Helena's history giving him a hint, that it was a suitable reward for kings to bestow upon fair ladies when they perform notable services.

Thus Helena at last found that her father's legacy was indeed sanctified by the luckiest stars in heaven; for she was now the beloved wife of her dear Bertram, the daughter-in-law of her noble mistress, and herself the Countess of Rousillon.

---

60 render ['rendər] (v.) 呈遞；提供

Lafeu　　I have seen a medicine
That's able to breathe life into a stone,
Quicken a rock, and make you dance canary
With spritely fire and motion, whose simple touch
Is powerful to araise King Pippen, nay
To give great Charlemain a pen in's hand
And write to her a love-line.
(II, i, 72-78)

拉福　　我剛看到一種藥，
能讓石子活起來，
能賦與岩塊生命，能使您翩然起舞
能讓您生龍活虎；它可以輕輕鬆鬆
讓培平大王復活，不只如此
還可以教查理曼大帝執起筆來，
為她寫下一行情詩。
（第二幕，第一景，72-78 行）

Countess If ever we are nature's, these are ours; this thorn
Doth to our rose of youth rightly belong;
Our blood to us, this to our blood is born;
It is the show and seal of nature's truth,
Where love's strong passion is impress'd in
    youth:
By our remembrances of days foregone,
Such were our faults, or then we thought them
    none.
(I, iii, 41-47)

伯爵夫人　我們是自然之子，擁有自然的感情；
這一根刺，是青春的薔薇上少不了的。
有了我們，就有感情；有了感情，就少不了這根刺。
當熱烈的愛戀烙印在青春裡，
這是自然天性的流露與痕跡。
在我們往日的回憶裡，我們會犯這樣錯，
而我們當時並不認為那有什麼不對。

（第一幕，第三景，41-47 行）

Measure for Measure

一報還一報

導讀

陳敬旻

故事來源

在十六世紀的歐洲，美貌女子被迫獻身以保全親人的性命是很常見的故事。《一報還一報》最主要的故事來源是英國劇作家匯斯東（George Whetstone）於 1578 年所著的《波莫思與卡珊卓》（*Promos and Cassandra*）。這個既不受歡迎也不曾演出的劇本，靈感得自於義大利的辛提歐（Giraldi Cinthio）所撰寫的《百則故事》（*Gli Hecatommithi*）。這兩位作者分別將這個故事寫了小說與戲劇兩種版本。莎翁根據這兩個版本，自創了瑪莉安娜一角，並決定讓公爵偽裝，且目睹整個事件的過程。

演出記錄

據記載， 1604 年本劇曾在英國國王詹姆士一世御前演出，當時為全新的劇作。 1603 年五月至隔年四月，倫敦的劇院因瘟疫被迫關閉，所以一般推測此劇完成的年代是 1604 年。

這齣戲雖然在第一版的莎翁全集第一對開本（the First Folio）裡被列為喜劇，但是直到最後「喜劇」收場為止，劇情的發展都缺乏喜劇感。

當此時期，是莎翁創作悲劇的登峰時期：他在 1603-4 年創作了《奧塞羅》， 1604-5 年寫就《李爾王》， 1606 年又推出《馬克白》。故依常理判斷，他應該不會在這段期間寫出如此受爭議的劇本，因此有部分學者認為，可能是莎翁自己在此時遭逢了人生的巨大創痛。

歷史紀錄顯示，本劇首演之後，經過了一甲子，才有機會重新搬演。而且這齣戲自十八世紀開始，一直到二十世紀為止，在舞台上的評價都不甚優良，劇本也鮮少獲得批評家的讚賞。

席德尼爵士（Sir Philip Sidney）也說：「喜劇就是模仿生活中的誤會，用最滑稽可笑的方式呈現，使觀眾認為絕對不可能發生。」從這兩個角度來看，稱《連環錯》為喜劇並不為過。莎士比亞似乎在他早期的劇場生涯就已經認為：歷經一連串的道德衝突或生命危險之後，達到圓滿結局，才算是喜劇收場。

負面評價

主要的原因是情節不合常理，結局又顯得突兀。 1754 年，藍納（Charlotte Lennox）曾將此劇和辛提歐的原作互相比較，並為文表示莎翁的改編愈改愈差，劇中只見「低等的計畫、荒謬的情節、不合情理的事件……為的就是讓一群人結婚，也不願以斬首作收。」

發表過眾多精闢莎劇見解的十九世紀文人兼批評家柯立芝（Coleridge），則稱此劇為「討厭的戲」，是莎翁「唯一令人痛苦的戲」。劇中的喜劇情節讓人生厭，悲劇情節讓人害怕：安哲羅可以說是犯了謀殺與強暴未遂兩項罪行，但劇終的正義卻完全只由寬恕取代；伊莎貝拉也不怎麼討人喜歡，她重視貞操的程度遠勝於親兄弟的性命；伊莎貝拉的弟弟則是個懦弱青年，自己犯錯卻期望姐姐犧牲貞操來換取自己的性命。

故事主題

劇中涉及諸多概念，包括道德、性慾、死亡、公權力的運用與濫用，以及人在關鍵時期所流露的本性及情感。本劇的劇名典出於新約馬太福音第七章：「不要審判，免得你們受審判。你們用什麼審判審判人，也必受什麼審判；你們用什麼量器量別人，也必用什麼量器被量。」如劇中，安哲羅即使魔高一尺，也終究要由道高一丈的公爵以其人之道，還治其人之身。

安哲羅雖然享有無瑕盛名，但當伊莎貝拉為被判死刑的弟弟求情時，他竟向伊莎貝拉提出以貞節作為換取條件，暴露他雙重的違法傾向——知法犯法（無夫妻之實而發生性行為者，依法必須處死），以及瀆職（因個人因素而未執行法律，使克勞狄免於一死）。然而一夜溫存之後，他又殘暴地下令將克勞狄處死，因而犯下了道義上的誑騙之罪和未婚性交的死罪。

但這一切並不證明他就是個不折不扣的偽君子，他為自己的色慾備受煎熬，一方面憎惡自己醜陋的罪行，另一方面又強烈受到純潔的伊莎貝拉所吸引，最後還受到一股莫名的力量驅使他殺害克勞狄，以掩飾自己的貪慾。事發之後，他也不求寬容，只想以死抵罪。但他就像《終成眷屬》的貝特漢及《無事生非》的克勞迪一樣，都犯下大錯，卻在劇終時獲得寬恕。

MEASURE FOR MEASURE.

伊莎貝拉和安哲羅雖然處於對立的立場，卻有巧合的雷同之處：崇尚精神與修行，過著與世隔絕的生活。安哲羅的行為與聲譽背道而馳，伊莎貝拉表裡如一，但她一樣無法獲得眾人的掌聲。一般人之所以對她不表示全然贊同，並不是因為她提倡慈悲或是矜持守節，而是因為性命不保的弟弟乞求她時，她仍給予無情的教訓。

伊莎貝拉在聖克萊兒修道院時，就希望院方能有更嚴謹的清規，事實上那已是羅馬天主教中最嚴格的教堂了。安哲羅要求她以身相報時，她被迫在「凜然赴死」與「含辱救弟」之間做一抉擇，她毫不考慮就選擇前者，並義正詞嚴教訓弟弟，甚至懷著仇恨似地要臨死的弟弟也應抱持相同的看法。

她和安哲羅一樣，對人性只有善惡對立的二分法。她請求公爵饒恕安哲羅，展現了高尚情操，但或許她並非懇求公爵原諒她的敵人，而是請求他饒瑪莉安娜的未婚夫一命。

偽裝成修道士的公爵，目睹純潔、沉淪和絕望的全部過程，然後在悲劇即將一發不可收拾之時，及時介入，挽救伊莎貝拉的貞節和克勞狄的性命。他還試驗他所觀察的人，如安哲羅、伊莎貝拉等，儼然像是無所不在的上帝。

公爵一角具有許多爭議：他愛民卻愛得不得其法，使得維也納城道
德敗壞；他怠忽職守卻不加以改進，反而決定由代理人安哲羅代為
導正，以逃避自己執法時可能遭致的批評及抗拒；他企圖操控所有
的角色，懷疑安哲羅只是「看似聖人」，似乎早料到他會出錯；克勞
狄即將處死，充滿恐懼，他卻只能提供基督教的思想教誨，勸誡他
平和安詳地告別這個世界；更令人不可置信的是，公爵竟然以「床
上把戲」（bed trick）做為解決方法，要瑪莉安娜代替伊莎貝拉與安
哲羅共度一夜，等於又犯下克勞狄與茱麗葉犯過的罪。因此，雖然
他在劇終時彷彿是從天而降的正義之神，對相關的人施予懲罰及寬
恕，但因代理事件而引發的種種痛苦、羞辱、憤怒與恐懼，他實則
要負最大的責任。

Escalus. Every letter he hath writ hath disvouched other.
Angelo. In most uneven and distracted manner.

Act IV. Scene IV.

大臣艾斯卡是本劇裡頭的折衷角色,他不像伊莎貝拉和安哲羅,對道德抱持極端嚴厲的態度,也不像公爵採取完全放任的立場。他的所作所為合情合理,以現實的眼光衡量事件的嚴重程度與處理方式,並以耐心和毅力解決政務問題。他贊成公爵的改革,又為克勞狄所處的境況求情。雖然如此,他沒有相對的權力執法,也無法使惡行因此而減少。法律規範期望的是能以外在的懲處,淨化內在的想法,而不應該一味要求人人都成為聖人,或永無止境地原諒罪人。

重新定位

時至二十世紀初，開始有批評家認為不應再以十九世紀自然主義的閱讀習慣來看待《一報還一報》，而應將其視為以戲劇面貌呈現的寓言故事，用以宣揚基督教高貴的精神。

少數不贊同上述說法的學者，紛紛將此劇歸類為「悲喜劇」（tragi-comedy），認為劇中的宗教意義、戲劇表現、人物塑造等等，都接近莎翁的戲劇風格及當時的民俗故事，而非單純的宣揚教義之作。

與莎翁同時期的人，也可能將《一報還一報》視為悲喜劇。義大利劇作家郭里尼（Giambattista Guarini）曾在 1601 年出版的著作《悲喜詩學概述》（*Compendium of Tragi-Comic Poetry*）中提到：悲喜劇是分別由悲劇與喜劇中擷取適當的成分，組合而成的第三種戲劇類型，具有悲劇的情節及險境，卻不包括悲劇的痛楚與死亡，同時又含有喜劇中的歡笑、娛樂、喜劇式逆轉和愉快結局。由開場時克勞狄的處境、伊莎貝拉的懇求或安哲羅的鐵石心腸來檢視本劇，將其歸為悲喜劇似乎並無不妥。

此外，當代也有評論家將此劇與《終成眷屬》一起視為「問題劇」（problem play）或「陰鬱喜劇」（dark comedy）。最早提出這個概念的是寶斯（F. S. Boas），他在 1896 年將此劇視為問題劇，並加以解釋：戲中營造的「不是全然的歡愉也非全然的痛苦，但我們卻為之振奮、著迷、困惑」，而劇中的問題，到最後也獲得令人滿意的結果。

Boy [*sings*]. Take, oh, take those lips away,
That so sweetly were forsworn.

Act IV. Scene I.

人物表

the duke	公爵	維也納一位公爵，後假扮成修士
Angelo	安哲羅	公爵的代理者
Claudio	克勞狄	因為被控誘拐女子而被關進監牢
Escalus	老臣艾斯卡	公爵的一位老臣
Lucio	陸西歐	克勞狄的友人
Isabel	伊莎貝拉	克勞狄的姊姊
Juliet	茱麗葉	克勞狄被控誘拐的女孩
Mariana	瑪莉安娜	安哲羅的未婚妻

Measure for Measure

In the city of Vienna there once reigned a duke of such a mild and gentle temper, that he suffered his subjects to neglect the laws with impunity[1]; and there was in particular one law, the existence of which was almost forgotten, the duke never having put it in force during his whole reign.

This was a law dooming any man to the punishment of death, who should live with a woman that was not his wife; and this law, through the lenity[2] of the duke, being utterly disregarded, the holy institution of marriage became neglected, and complaints were every day made to the duke by the parents of the young ladies in Vienna, that their daughters had been seduced[3] from their protection, and were living as the companions of single men.

The good duke perceived with sorrow this growing evil among his subjects; but he thought that a sudden change in himself from the indulgence he had hitherto shown, to the strict severity requisite[4] to check this abuse, would make his people (who had hitherto loved him) consider him as a tyrant.

1 impunity [ɪmˈpjuːnɪti] (n.) 免受懲罰
2 lenity [ˈlenəti] (n.) 〔正式〕慈悲；寬厚
3 seduce [sɪˈdjuːs] (v.) 勾引；誘姦
4 requisite [ˈrekwɪzɪt] (a.) 需要的；必要的

 Therefore he determined to absent himself a while from his dukedom, and depute[5] another to the full exercise of his power, that the law against these dishonorable lovers might be put in effect, without giving offense by an unusual severity in his own person.

Angelo, a man who bore the reputation of a saint in Vienna for his strict and rigid life, was chosen by the duke as a fit person to undertake this important charge; and when the duke imparted[6] his design to Lord Escalus, his chief counselor, Escalus said, "If any man in Vienna be of worth to undergo such ample grace and honor, it is Lord Angelo."

5 depute [dɪˈpjuːt] (v.) 將（工作、職權等）交予代理人
6 impart [ɪmˈpɑːrt] (v.) 〔正式〕通知；告知

🎧 **32** And now the duke departed from Vienna under pretense of making a journey into Poland, leaving Angelo to act as the lord deputy in his absence; but the duke's absence was only a feigned one, for he privately returned to Vienna, habited like a friar[7], with the intent to watch unseen the conduct of the saintly-seeming Angelo.

It happened just about the time that Angelo was invested with his new dignity, that a gentleman, whose name was Claudio, had seduced a young lady from her parents; and for this offense, by command of the new lord deputy, Claudio was taken up and committed to prison, and by virtue of the old law which had been so long neglected, Angelo sentenced Claudio to be be-headed.

Great interest was made for the pardon of young Claudio, and the good old Lord Escalus himself interceded[8] for him. "Alas," said he, "this gentleman whom I would save had an honorable father, for whose sake I pray you pardon the young man's transgression[9]."

---

7 friar ['fraɪər] (n.) 修道士
8 intercede [ˌɪntərˈsiːd] (v.) （為調停或為獲得贊助而）說項；求情
9 transgression [trænsˈgreʃən] (n.) 逾越；違犯；道德犯罪

🎧33 But Angelo replied, "We must not make a scarecrow[10] of the law, setting it up to frighten birds of prey, till custom, finding it harmless, makes it their perch[11], and not their terror. Sir, he must die."

Lucio, the friend of Claudio, visited him in the prison, and Claudio said to him, "I pray you, Lucio, do me this kind service. Go to my sister Isabel, who this day proposes to enter the convent[12] of Saint Clare; acquaint her with the danger of my state; implore her that she make friends with the strict deputy; bid her go herself to Angelo. I have great hopes in that; for she can discourse with prosperous art, and well she can persuade; besides, there is a speechless dialect in youthful sorrow, such as moves men."

---

10 scarecrow ['skerkroʊ] (n.)（置於農作物中用來嚇走鳥類的）人形；稻草人

11 perch [pɜːtʃ] (n.) 鳥的棲息之所（如樹枝）；棲木

12 convent ['kɑːnvent] (n.)（與塵世隔絕以侍奉上帝的）女修道會；修女會

🎧34   Isabel, the sister of Claudio, had, as he said, that day entered upon her novitiate[13] in the convent, and it was her intent, after passing through her probation[14] as a novice[15], to take the veil, and she was inquiring of a nun concerning the rules of the convent, when they heard the voice of Lucio, who, as he entered that religious house, said, "Peace be in this place!"

"Who is it that speaks?" said Isabel.

"It is a man's voice," replied the nun: "Gentle Isabel, go to him, and learn his business; you may, I may not. When you have taken the veil, you must not speak with men but in the presence of the prioress[16]; then if you speak you must not show your face, or if you show your face, you must not speak."

"And have you nuns no further privileges?" said Isabel.

"Are not these large enough?" replied the nun.

"Yes, truly," said Isabel: "I speak not as desiring more, but rather wishing a more strict restraint upon the sisterhood, the votarists[17] of Saint Clare."

---

13 novitiate [nouˈvɪʃɪət] (n.) 做見習修士或修女；見習期
14 probation [prouˈbeɪʃən] (n.)（給予某人一職位、准許某人加入某
                  會社等之前的）試用
15 novice [ˈnɑːvɪs] (n.) 生手；初學者；（尤指）見習修士或修女
16 prioress [ˈpraɪərɪs] (n.) 小女修道院院長
17 votarist [ˈvoutərɪst] (n.) 熱心者；支持（尤指宗教工作）者

Again they heard the voice of Lucio, and the nun said, "He calls again. I pray you answer him."

Isabel then went out to Lucio, and in answer to his salutation, said, "Peace and Prosperity! Who is it that calls?"

Then Lucio, approaching her with reverence, said, "Hail[18], virgin, if such you be, as the roses on your cheeks proclaim you are no less! can you bring me to the sight of Isabel, a novice of this place, and the fair sister to her unhappy brother Claudio?"

Lucio. Gentle and fair, your brother kindly greets you.
Not to be weary with you, he's in prison.
Isabella. Woe me! for what?   Act I. Scene V.

"Why her unhappy brother?" said Isabel, "let me ask! for I am that Isabel, and his sister."

"Fair and gentle lady," he replied, "your brother kindly greets you by me; he is in prison."

"Woe[19] is me! for what?" said Isabel.

---

18 hail [heɪl] (v.) 歡迎；向……招呼（以引其注意）
19 woe [woʊ] (n.) 悲哀；悲痛；痛苦

🎧 36 Lucio then told her, Claudio was imprisoned for seducing a young maiden.

"Ah," said she, "I fear it is my cousin Juliet."

Juliet and Isabel were not related, but they called each other cousin in remembrance of their school days' friendship; and as Isabel knew that Juliet loved Claudio, she feared she had been led by her affection for him into this transgression.

"She it is," replied Lucio.

"Why, then, let my brother marry Juliet," said Isabel.

Lucio replied that Claudio would gladly marry Juliet, but that the lord deputy had sentenced him to die for his offense. "Unless," said he, "you have the grace by your fair prayer to soften Angelo, and that is my business between you and your poor brother."

"Alas!" said Isabel, "what poor ability is there in me to do him good? I doubt I have no power to move Angelo."

"Our doubts are traitors," said Lucio, "and make us lose the good we might often win, by fearing to attempt it. Go to Lord Angelo! When maidens sue, and kneel, and weep, men give like gods."

"I will see what I can do", said Isabel: "I will but stay to give the prioress notice of the affair, and then I will go to Angelo. Commend me to my brother: soon at night I will send him word of my success."

Isabel hastened to the palace, and threw herself on her knees before Angelo, saying, "I am a woeful suitor to your honor, if it will please your honor to hear me."

"Well, what is your suit?" said Angelo.

She then made her petition in the most moving terms for her brother's life.

But Angelo said, "Maiden, there is no remedy; your brother is sentenced, and he must die."

"Oh just, but severe law," said Isabel: "I had a brother then— heaven keep your honor!" and she was about to depart.

🎧38 But Lucio, who had accompanied her, said, "Give it not over so; return to him again, entreat him, kneel down before him, hang upon his gown. You are too cold; if you should need a pin, you could not with a more tame tongue desire it."

Then again Isabel on her knees implored for mercy.

"He is sentenced," said Angelo: "It is too late."

"Too late!" said Isabel. "Why, no! I that do speak a word may call it back again. Believe this, my lord, no ceremony that to great ones belongs, not the king's crown, nor the deputed sword, the marshal's [20] truncheon [21], nor the judge's robe, becomes them with one half so good a grace as mercy does."

"Pray you begone," said Angelo.

But still Isabel entreated; and she said, "If my brother had been as you, and you as he, you might have slipped like him, but he, like you, would not have been so stern. I would to heaven I had your power, and you were Isabel. Should it then be thus? No, I would tell you what it were to be a judge, and what a prisoner."

---

20 marshal ['mɑːrʃəl] (n.) 最高級軍官；元帥
21 truncheon ['trʌnʃən] (n.) 官杖；司令杖

"Be content, fair maid!" said Angelo: "it is the law, not I, condemns your brother. Were he my kinsman, my brother, or my son, it should be thus with him. He must die tomorrow."

"Tomorrow?" said Isabel. "Oh, that is sudden: spare him, spare him; he is not prepared for death. Even for our kitchens we kill the fowl in season; shall we serve Heaven with less respect than we minister to our gross selves? Good, good, my lord, bethink you, none have died for my brother's offense, though many have committed it. So you would be the first that gives this sentence, and he the first that suffers it. Go

to your own bosom, my lord; knock there, and ask your heart what it does know that is like my brother's fault; if it confess a natural guiltiness such as his is, let it not sound a thought against my brother's life!"

🎧40 Her last words more moved Angelo than all she had before said, for the beauty of Isabel had raised a guilty passion in his heart, and he began to form thoughts of dishonorable love, such as Claudio's crime had been; and the conflict in his mind made him to turn away from Isabel; but she called him back, saying, "Gentle my lord, turn back; hark[22], how I will bribe you. Good my lord, turn back!"

"How, bribe me?" said Angelo, astonished that she should think of offering him a bribe.

"Ay," said Isabel, "with such gifts that heaven itself shall share with you; not with golden treasures, or those glittering stones, whose price is either rich or poor as fancy values them, but with true prayers that shall be up to heaven before sunrise— prayers from preserved souls, from fasting[23] maids whose minds are dedicated to nothing temporal[24]."

22 hark [hɑːrk] (v.) 〔俗〕〔揶揄〕聽
23 fasting ['fæstɪŋ] 禁食的；齋戒的
24 temporal ['tempərəl] (a.) 世俗的；現世的；非精神生活的

"Well, come to me tomorrow," said Angelo.

And for this short respite[25] of her brother's life, and for this permission that she might be heard again, she left him with the joyful hope that she should at last prevail over his stern nature: and as she went away she said: "Heaven keep your honor safe! Heaven save your honor!" Which when Angelo heard, he said within his heart, "Amen, I would be saved from thee and from thy virtues."

And then, affrighted at his own evil thoughts, he said, "What is this? What is this? Do I love her, that I desire to hear her speak again, and feast upon her eyes? What is it I dream on? The cunning enemy of mankind, to catch a saint, with saints does bait the hook. Never could an immodest woman once stir my temper, but this virtuous woman subdues[26] me quite. Even till now, when men were fond, I smiled and wondered at them."

---

25 respite [ˈrespɪt] (n.) 刑罰或義務之展延；暫緩行刑
26 subdue [səbˈduː] (v.) 征服；克服

In the guilty conflict in his mind Angelo suffered more that night than the prisoner he had so severely sentenced; for in the prison Claudio was visited by the good duke, who, in his friar's habit, taught the young man the way to heaven, preaching to him the words of penitence[27] and peace.

But Angelo felt all the pangs of irresolute guilt: now wishing to seduce Isabel from the paths of innocence and honor, and now suffering remorse and horror for a crime as yet but intentional. But in the end his evil thoughts prevailed; and he who had so lately started at the offer of a bribe, resolved to tempt this maiden with so high a bribe, as she might not be able to resist, even with the precious gift of her dear brother's life.

27 penitence ['penɪtəns] (n.) 懺悔；後悔（所犯之錯或罪）

When Isabel came in the morning, Angelo desired she might be admitted alone to his presence: and being there he said to her, if she would yield to him her virgin honor and transgress even as Juliet had done with Claudio, he would give her her brother's life.

"For," said he, "I love you, Isabel."

"My brother," said Isabel, "did so love Juliet, and yet you tell me he shall die for it."

"But," said Angelo, "Claudio shall not die, if you will consent to visit me by stealth at night, even as Juliet left her father's house at night to come to Claudio."

Isabel, in amazement at his words, that he should tempt her to the same fault for which he passed sentence upon her brother, said, "I would do as much for my poor brother as for myself; that is, were I under sentence of death, the impression of keen whips[28] I would wear as rubies, and go to my death as to a bed that longing I had been sick for, ere[29] I would yield myself up to this shame." And then she told him, she hoped he only spoke these words to try her virtue.

---

28 whip [wɪp] (n.) 鞭打
29 ere [er] (adv.) 〔舊〕〔法〕〔詩〕在前；在……之前

🎧44 But he said, "Believe me, on my honor, my words express my purpose."

Isabel, angered to the heart to hear him use the word Honor to express such dishonorable purposes; said, "Ha! little honor to be much believed; and most pernicious[30] purpose. I will proclaim thee, Angelo, look for it! Sign me a present pardon for my brother, or I will tell the world aloud what man thou art!"

"Who will believe you, Isabel?" said Angelo; "my unsoiled name, the austereness[31] of my life, my word vouched[32] against yours, will outweigh your accusation. Redeem your brother by yielding to my will, or he shall die tomorrow. As for you, say what you can, my false will overweigh your true story. Answer me tomorrow."

Isabella. I will proclaim thee, Angelo, look for't.
Act II. Scene IV.

---

30 pernicious [pər'nɪʃəs] (a.) （對……）有害的；傷害性的
31 austereness [ɔː'stɪrnɪs] (n.) 嚴肅；樸素
32 vouch [vautʃ] (v.) 保證；擔保

"To whom should I complain? Did I tell this, who would believe me?" said Isabel, as she went towards the dreary prison where her brother was confined[33]. When she arrived there, her brother was in pious conversation with the duke, who in his friar's habit had also visited Juliet and brought both these guilty lovers to a proper sense of their fault; and unhappy Juliet with tears and a true remorse confessed that she was more to blame than Claudio, in that she willingly consented to his dishonorable solicitations.

As Isabel entered the room where Claudio was confined, she said, "Peace be here, grace, and good company!"

"Who is there?" said the disguised duke. "Come in; the wish deserves a welcome."

---

33 confine [kən'faɪn] (v.) 關起來；禁閉

🎧 46 "My business is a word or two with Claudio," said Isabel.

Then the duke left them together, and desired the provost, who had the charge of the prisoners, to place him where he might overhear their conversation.

"Now, sister, what is the comfort?" said Claudio.

Isabel told him he must prepare for death on the morrow.

"Is there no remedy?" said Claudio.

"Yes, brother," replied Isabel, "there is; but such a one as, if you consented to it would strip your honor from you, and leave you naked."

"Let me know the point," said Claudio.

"Oh, I do fear you, Claudio!" replied his sister; "and I quake, lest you should wish to live, and more respect the trifling term of six or seven winters added to your life, than your perpetual honor! Do you dare to die? The sense of death is most in apprehension[34], and the poor beetle that we tread upon, feels a pang as great as when a giant dies."

---

34 apprehension [ˌæprɪˈhenʃən] (n.) 恐懼;憂慮

"Why do you give me this shame?" said Claudio. "Think you I can fetch a resolution from flowery tenderness? If I must die, I will encounter darkness as a bride, and hug it in my arms."

"There spoke my brother," said Isabel; "there my father's grave did utter forth a voice. Yes, you must die; yet would you think it, Claudio! this outward sainted deputy, if I would yield to him my virgin honor, would grant your life. Oh, were it but my life, I would lay it down for your deliverance as frankly as a pin!"

"Thanks, dear Isabel," said Claudio.

"Be ready to die tomorrow," said Isabel.

"Death is a fearful thing," said Claudio.

"And shamed life a hateful," replied his sister.

But the thoughts of death now overcame the constancy of Claudio's temper, and terrors, such as the guilty only at their deaths do know, assailing[35] him, he cried out, "Sweet sister, let me live! The sin you do to save a brother's life, nature dispenses[36] with the deed so far, that it becomes a virtue."

35 assail [əˈseɪl] (v.) 猛擊；痛擊；困擾
36 dispense [dɪˈspens] (v.) 赦免；寬恕

Claudio.   O Isabel !
Isabella.   What says my brother?
Claudio.   Death is a fearful thing
                                        Act III.   Scene I.

"Oh faithless coward! Oh dishonest wretch[37]!" said Isabel. "Would you preserve your life by your sister's shame? Oh, fie[38], fie, fie! I thought, my brother, you had in you such a mind of honor, that had you twenty heads to render up on twenty blocks, you would have yielded them up all before your sister should stoop to such dishonor."

"Nay, hear me, Isabel!" said Claudio.

But what he would have said in defense of his weakness, in desiring to live by the dishonor of his virtuous sister, was interrupted by the entrance of the duke.

37 wretch [retʃ] (n.) 卑鄙的人
38 fie [faɪ] (interj.) （通常為詼諧語）呸！

49   Who said, "Claudio, I have overheard what has passed between you and your sister. Angelo had never the purpose to corrupt her; what he said, has only been to make trial of her virtue. She having the truth of honor in her, has given him that gracious denial which he is most glad to receive. There is no hope that he will pardon you; therefore pass your hours in prayer, and make ready for death."

Then Claudio repented of his weakness, and said: "Let me ask my sister's pardon! I am so out of love with life, that I will sue to be rid of it." And Claudio retired, overwhelmed with shame and sorrow for his fault.

The duke being now alone with Isabel, commended her virtuous resolution, saying, "The hand that made you fair, has made you good."

"Oh," said Isabel, "how much is the good duke deceived in Angelo! If ever he return, and I can speak to him, I will discover his government." Isabel knew not that she was even now making the discovery she threatened.

The duke replied, "That shall not be much amiss; yet as the matter now stands, Angelo will repel[39] your accusation; therefore lend an attentive ear to my advisings. I believe that you may most righteously do a poor wronged lady a merited benefit, redeem your brother from the angry law, do no stain to your own most gracious person, and much please the absent duke, if peradventure[40] he shall ever return to have notice of this business."

Isabel said, she had a spirit to do anything he desired, provided it was nothing wrong.

"Virtue is bold, and never fearful," said the duke: and then he asked her, if she had ever heard of Mariana, the sister of Frederick, the great soldier who was drowned at sea.

"I have heard of the lady," said Isabel, "and good words went with her name."

---

39 repel [rɪ'pel] (v.) 逐退
40 peradventure [ˌpɜːrəd'ventʃər] (adv.) 偶爾；萬一

🎧 51　"This lady," said the duke, "is the wife of Angelo; but her marriage dowry[41] was on board the vessel in which her brother perished, and mark how heavily this befell to the poor gentlewoman! for, beside the loss of a most noble and renowned brother, who in his love towards her was ever most kind and natural, in the wreck[42] of her fortune she lost the affections of her husband, the well-seeming Angelo; who pretending to discover some dishonor in this honorable lady (though the true cause was the loss of her dowry) left her in her tears, and dried not one of them with his comfort. His unjust unkindness, that in all reason should have quenched[43] her love, has, like an impediment[44] in the current, made it more unruly[45], and Mariana loves her cruel husband with the full continuance of her first affection."

The duke then more plainly unfolded his plan. It was, that Isabel should go to Lord Angelo, and seemingly consent to come to him as he desired at midnight; that by this means she would obtain the promised pardon; and that Mariana should go in her stead to the appointment, and pass herself upon Angelo in the dark for Isabel.

41　dowry ['daʊri] (n.) 嫁妝；陪嫁物
42　wreck [rek] (n.)（尤指船遭受暴風雨襲擊所造成的）船難；失事
43　quench [kwentʃ] (v.) 結束；滅絕（希望）
44　impediment [ɪm'pedɪmənt] (n.) 障礙物；障礙
45　unruly [ʌn'ruːli] (n.) 難控制的

Mariana

"Nor, gentle daughter," said the feigned friar, "fear you to do this thing; Angelo is her husband, and to bring them thus together is no sin."

Isabel being pleased with this project, departed to do as he directed her; and he went to apprise[46] Mariana of their intention. He had before this time visited this unhappy lady in his assumed character, giving her religious instruction and friendly consolation, at which times he had learned her sad story from her own lips; and now she, looking upon him as a holy man, readily consented to be directed by him in this undertaking.

When Isabel returned from her interview with Angelo, to the house of Mariana, where the duke had appointed her to meet him, he said, "Well met, and in good time; what is the news from this good deputy?"

Isabel related the manner in which she had settled the affair. "Angelo," said she, "has a garden surrounded with a brick wall, on the western side of which is a vineyard, and to that vineyard is a gate."

46 apprise [əˈpraɪz] (n.) 〔正式〕通知；報告

53 And then she showed to the duke and Mariana two keys that Angelo had given her; and she said, "This bigger key opens the vineyard gate; this other a little door which leads from the vineyard to the garden. There I have made my promise at the dead of the night to call upon him, and have got from him his word of assurance for my brother's life. I have taken a due and wary[47] note of the place; and with whispering and most guilty diligence he showed me the way twice over."

"Are there no other tokens agreed upon between you, that Mariana must observe?" said the duke.

"No, none," said Isabel, "only to go when it is dark. I have told him my time can be but short; for I have made him think a servant comes along with me, and that this servant is persuaded I come about my brother."

---

47 wary ['wεri] (a.) 小心地；慣於留神可能的危機或困難的

The duke commended her discreet management, and she, turning to Mariana, said, "Little have you to say to Angelo, when you depart from him, but soft and low, *remember now my brother!*"

Mariana was that night conducted to the appointed place by Isabel, who rejoiced that she had, as she supposed, by this device preserved both her brother's life and her own honor.

But that her brother's life was safe the duke was not well satisfied, and therefore at midnight he again repaired to the prison, and it was well for Claudio that he did so, else would Claudio have that night been beheaded; for soon after the duke entered the prison, an order came from the cruel deputy, commanding that Claudio should be beheaded, and his head sent to him by five o'clock in the morning.

But the duke persuaded the provost to put off the execution of Claudio, and to deceive Angelo, by sending him the head of a man who died that morning in the prison.

🎧55 And to prevail upon the provost to agree to this, the duke, whom still the provost suspected not to be anything more or greater than he seemed, showed the provost a letter written with the duke's hand, and sealed with his seal, which when the provost saw, he concluded this friar must have some secret order from the absent duke, and therefore he consented to spare Claudio; and he cut off the dead man's head and carried it to Angelo.

Then the duke, in his own name, wrote to Angelo a letter, saying that certain accidents had put a stop to his journey, and that he should be in Vienna by the following morning, requiring Angelo to meet him at the entrance of the city, there to deliver up his authority; and the duke also commanded it to be proclaimed, that if any of his subjects craved redress for injustice, they should exhibit their petitions in the street on his first entrance into the city.

Early in the morning Isabel came to the prison, and the duke, who there awaited her coming, for secret reasons thought it good to tell her that Claudio was beheaded; therefore when Isabel inquired if Angelo had sent the pardon for her brother, he said, "Angelo has released Claudio from this world. His head is off, and sent to the deputy."

The much-grieved sister cried out, "Oh unhappy Claudio, wretched Isabel, injurious world, most wicked Angelo!"

The seeming friar bid her take comfort, and when she was become a little calm, he acquainted her with the near prospect of the duke's return, and told her in what manner she should proceed in preferring her complaint against Angelo; and he bade her not fear if the cause should seem to go against her for a while. Leaving Isabel sufficiently instructed, he next went to Mariana, and gave her counsel in what manner she also should act.

Then the duke laid aside his friar's habit, and in his own royal robes, amid a joyful crowd of his faithful subjects, assembled to greet his arrival, entered the city of Vienna, where he was met by Angelo, who delivered up his authority in the proper form.

🎧 57 And there came Isabel, in the manner of a petitioner for redress, and said, "Justice, most royal duke! I am the sister of one Claudio, who, for the seducing a young maid, was condemned to lose his head. I made my suit to Lord Angelo for my brother's pardon. It were needless to tell your grace how I prayed and kneeled, how he repelled me, and how I replied; for this was of much length. The vile conclusion I now begin with grief and shame to utter. Angelo would not, but by my yielding to his dishonorable love release my brother; and after much debate within myself, my sisterly remorse overcame my virtue, and I did yield to him. But the next morning betimes, Angelo, forfeiting his promise, sent a warrant for my poor brother's head!"

The duke affected[48] to disbelieve her story; and Angelo said that grief for her brother's death, who had suffered by the due course of the law, had disordered her senses.

---

48 affect [əˈfɛkt] (v.) 佯為；假裝

58   And now another suitor approached, which was Mariana; and Mariana said, "Noble prince, as there comes light from heaven, and truth from breath, as there is sense in truth and truth in virtue, I am this man's wife, and, my good lord, the words of Isabel are false; for the night she says she was with Angelo, I passed that night with him in the garden-house. As this is true, let me in safety rise, or else forever be fixed here a marble monument."

🎧59 Then did Isabel appeal for the truth of what she had said to Friar Lodowick, that being the name the duke had assumed in his disguise.

Isabel and Mariana had both obeyed his instructions in what they said, the duke intending that the innocence of Isabel should be plainly proved in that public manner before the whole city of Vienna; but Angelo little thought that it was from such a cause that they thus differed in their story, and he hoped from their contradictory evidence to be able to clear himself from the accusation of Isabel; and he said, assuming the look of offended innocence:

"I did but smile till now; but, good my lord, my patience here is touched, and I perceive these poor, distracted women are but the instruments of some greater one, who sets them on. Let me have way, my lord, to find this practice out."

"Ay, with all my heart," said the duke, "and punish them to the height of your pleasure. You, Lord Escalus, sit with Lord Angelo, lend him your pains to discover this abuse; the friar is sent for that set them on, and when he comes, do with your injuries as may seem best in any chastisement[49]. I for a while will leave you, but stir not you, Lord Angelo, till you have well determined upon this slander[50]."

---

49 chastisement [tʃæsˈtaɪzmənt] (n.) 懲罰
50 slander [ˈslændər] (n.) 毀謗；毀謗罪

🎧 60 The duke then went away, leaving Angelo well pleased to be deputed judge and umpire in his own cause.

But the duke was absent only while he threw off his royal robes and put on his friar's habit; and in that disguise again he presented himself before Angelo and Escalus: and the good old Escalus, who thought Angelo had been falsely accused, said to the supposed friar, "Come, sir, did you set these women on to slander Lord Angelo?"

He replied, "Where is the duke? It is he who should hear me speak."

Escalus said, "The duke is in us, and we will hear you. Speak justly."

"Boldly, at least," retorted[51] the friar; and then he blamed the duke for leaving the cause of Isabel in the hands of him she had accused, and spoke so freely of many corrupt practices he had observed, while, as he said, he had been a looker-on in Vienna, that Escalus threatened, him with the torture for speaking words against the state, and for censuring the conduct of the duke, and ordered him to be taken away to prison. Then, to the amazement of all present, and to the utter confusion of Angelo, the supposed friar threw off his disguise, and they saw it was the duke himself.

51 retort [rɪˈtɔːrt] (v.)（尤指對控訴或挑戰）立即機智或憤怒地反駁

The duke first addressed Isabel. He said to her, "Come hither, Isabel. Your friar is now your prince, but with my habit I have not changed my heart. I am still devoted to your service."

"Oh, give me pardon," said Isabel, "that I, your vassal, have employed and troubled your unknown sovereignty."

He answered that he had most need of forgiveness from her, for not having prevented the death of her brother— for not yet would he tell her that Claudio was living; meaning first to make a further trial of her goodness.

Angelo now knew the duke had been a secret witness of his bad deeds, and be said, "Oh my dread lord, I should be guiltier than my guiltiness, to think I can be undiscernible[52], when I perceive your grace, like power divine, has looked upon my actions. Then, good prince, no longer prolong my shame, but let my trial be my own confession. Immediate sentence and death is all the grace I beg."

---

52 undiscernible [ˌʌndɪˈsɜːrnɪbəl] (a.) 不受辨明的；不被認清的

Act. 5 Scene 1.

LUCIO.
Show your knave's visage, with a pox to you!
show your sheep-biting face, and be hanged an hour! Will't not off?

🎧62 　The duke replied, "Angelo, thy faults are manifest.
We do condemn thee to the very block where Claudio
stooped to death; and with like haste away with him;
and for his possessions, Mariana, we do instate and
widow you withal[53], to buy you a better husband."

　"Oh my dear lord," said Mariana, "I crave[54] no other,
nor no better man!" And then on her knees, even as
Isabel had begged the life of Claudio, did this kind
wife of an ungrateful husband beg the life of Angelo;
and she said, "Gentle my liege[55], O good my lord!
Sweet Isabel, take my part! Lend me your knees, and
all my life to come I will lend you all my life, to do you
service!"

53　withal [wɪˈðɔːl] (adv.)〔古〕且；此外
54　crave [kreɪv] (v.) 懇求；渴望
55　liege [liːdʒ] (n.) 君主；王侯

121

MARIANA.   My husband bids me; now I will unmask.

🎧 63 The duke said, "Against all sense you importune[56] her. Should Isabel kneel down to beg for mercy, her brother's ghost would break his paved bed, and take her hence in horror."

Still Mariana said, "Isabel, sweet Isabel, do but kneel by me, hold up your hand, say nothing! I will speak all. They say, best men are molded out of faults, and for the most part become much the better for being a little bad. So may my husband. Oh, Isabel! will you not lend a knee?"

---

56 importune [ˌɪmpərˈtuːn] (v.) 再三要求；不斷請求

🎧64 The duke then said, "He dies for Claudio."

But much pleased was the good duke, when his own Isabel, from whom he expected all gracious and honorable acts, kneeled down before him, and said, "Most bounteous[57] sir, look, if it please you, on this man condemned, as if my brother lived. I partly think a due sincerity governed his deeds, till he did look on me. Since it is so, let him not die! My brother had but justice, in that he did the thing for which he died."

The duke, as the best reply he could make to this noble petitioner for her enemy's life, sending for Claudio from his prison-house, where he lay doubtful of his destiny, presented to her this lamented brother living; and he said to Isabel, "Give me your hand, Isabel; for your lovely sake I pardon Claudio. Say you will be mine, and he shall be my brother, too."

By this time Lord Angelo perceived he was safe and the duke, observing his eye to brighten up a little, said, "Well, Angelo, look that you love your wife; her worth has obtained your pardon. Joy to you, Mariana! Love her, Angelo! I have confessed her, and know her virtue."

---

57 bounteous ['bauntiəs] (a.) 〔文〕慷慨的；豐富的

🎧 65 Angelo remembered, when dressed in a little brief authority, how hard his heart had been, and felt how sweet is mercy.

The duke commanded Claudio to marry Juliet, and offered himself again to the acceptance of Isabel, whose virtuous and noble conduct had won her prince's heart.

Isabel, not having taken the veil, was free to marry; and the friendly offices, while hid under the disguise of a humble friar, which the noble duke had done for her, made her with grateful joy accept the honor he offered her; and when she became Duchess of Vienna, the excellent example of the virtuous Isabel worked such a complete reformation among the young ladies of that city, that from that time none ever fell into the transgression of Juliet, the repentant wife of the reformed Claudio. And the mercy-loving duke long reigned with his beloved Isabel, the happiest of husbands and of princes.

Quotation
Measure for Measure

Isabella　　But man, proud man,
Dress'd in a little brief authority,
Most ignorant of what he's most assur'd
His glassy essence.
(II, ii, 117-20)

伊莎貝拉　　可是，人，驕傲的人，
掌握到一點點短暫的權威，
就會把自己萬分確定的事忘得一乾二淨──
那就是他玻璃易碎的本質。
（第二幕，第二景，117-20 行）

國家圖書館出版品預行編目資料

悅讀莎士比亞故事 .8, 終成眷屬 & 一報還一報 / Charles and Mary Lamb 著 ; Cosmos Language Workshop　譯 . 一初版 . 一 [臺北市] : 寂天文化 , 2012.6　面 ; 公分 .

ISBN　978-986-318-007-4　(25K 平裝附光碟片)

1. 英語　　　2. 讀本

805.18　　　　　　　　　　　　　　　101010088

作者	Charles and Mary Lamb
譯者	Cosmos Language Workshop
編輯	陸葵珍
主編	黃鈺云
內文排版	陸葵珍
製程管理	蔡智堯
出版者	寂天文化事業股份有限公司
電話	02-2365-9739
傳真	02-2365-9835
網址	www.icosmos.com.tw
讀者服務	onlineservice@icosmos.com.tw
出版日期	2012 年 6 月 初版一刷 (250101)
	版權所有 請勿翻印
郵撥帳號	1998620-0 寂天文化事業股份有限公司
	訂購金額 600 (含) 元以上郵資免費
	訂購金額 600 元以下者，請外加郵資 60 元

CONTENTS

1 Postreading

1. Are you for or against the idea that a woman woos a man? Why?

2. Do you think it's useful or necessary to achieve your end by setting up a device?

2 Vocabulary

A. Fill in the blanks with the words from the following list.

cordial	discreet	disposition
hazarded	observance	prevailed

1. The countess praised the virtuous _____ and excellent qualities of Helena.

2. Helena had many difficulties to encounter, for the king was not easily _____ on to try the medicine offered him by this fair young doctor.

3. Though Helena gained the noble husband she had _____ her life to obtain, she seemed to have won but a splendid blank.

4. I am your most obedient servant, and shall ever with true _____ seek to eke out that desert, wherein my homely stars have failed to equal my great fortunes

5. The good countess received her with a _____ welcome, as if she had been her son's own choice, and a lady of a high degree.

6. All this the good lady related to Helena, highly praising the virtuous principles of her _____ daughter.

B. Read the following sentences and write down the meanings of the underlined words.

1. When you are not in a good mood, you like to listen to some nice music to <u>sooth</u> your troubled mind.
   Sooth means _____.
2. You <u>inherited</u> the looks from your parents, so you look like them. **Inherit** means _____ .
3. Your principal announced that no student is allowed to have his or her hair dyed. Some students think it's unreasonable and are writing a <u>petition</u> to the principal.
   Petition means _____ .
4. You are not interested in a subject at all, but your teacher <u>compels</u> you to study it.
   Compel means _____ .

3 | Identification

Bertram	Helena	Countess of Rousillon
Diana	Lafeu	Gerard de Narbon
the Widow	King of France	

A. Who are they? Fill in the blanks with the characters from the following list.

1. _____ A young gentlewoman who doubly won Bertram as her husband with her conceived projects.
2. _____ A very hospitable lady who used to receive into her house the female pilgrims that were going to visit the shrine of St. Jaques le Grand.
3. _____ A fair young lady who was the daughter of the widow and was loved by Bertram.

B. Who said or did these?

1. _____ "Love is a thorn that belongs to the rose of youth; for in the season of youth, if ever we are nature's children,

these faults are ours, though then we think not they are faults."

2. _____ "My lord your son made me to think of this; else Paris, and the medicine, and the king, had from the conversation of my thoughts been absent then."

3. _____ "When you can get the ring from my finger, which never shall come off, then call me husband, but in such a Then I write a Never."

4. _____ "My good lady, I have forgiven and forgotten all."

5. _____ "This I must say, the young lord did great offence to his majesty, his mother, and his lady; but to himself he did the greatest wrong of all."

4 Comprehension: Choose the correct answer.

___ 1. Why did the king of France send for Bertram to come immediately to his royal court in Paris?
   a) He used to be full of affection for the countess, so for the great affliction she brought him when she married the late count, he intended to get revenge on their son.
   b) He loved the father of Bertram, for the friendship he bore the late count, he intended to grace young Bertram with his especial favor and protection.
   c) He had a beloved fair daughter who was a young maid, whom he intended to marry Bertram.
   d) He was completely occupied by the complex state affairs, for which reason he intended to call for help from Bertram.

___ 2. What was Helena's father Gerard de Narbon?
   a) He was a count.   b) He was a pilgrim.
   c) He was a magician.   d) He was a physician.

___ 3. For whom did the tears Helena shed for when Bertram was leaving for Paris?
   a) The king, for he had fallen into an incurable malady.
   b) The countess, for she seemed a second time to bury her husband.
   c) Bertram, for she had long loved him.

4

d) Gerard de Narbon, for the memory of his paternal love for her.

_____ 4. Why did not Helena profess her strong love to Bertram?
    a) She always remembered that he was descended from the most ancient family in France. She of humble birth.
    b) She knew that Bertram's heart was filled with the Diana.
    c) He said she was a poor physician's daughter, bred at his father's charge, and now living a dependent on his mother's bounty.
    d) Bertram had been brought up under the counsels of the prudent countess, who insisted that he should marry a lady of a high degree.

_____ 5. How did Helena win Bertram at the first time?
    a) By curing the king who promised to give her a husband at her own choice. She chose him to be her husband.
    b) By following Bertram to Paris and professed her love for him. He was very much moved by her words.
    c) By imploring the countess to grant their marriage. The countess agreed to her proposal.
    d) By requesting her hostess and her daughter to allow her to pass herself upon Bertram for Diana. She got the ring from him.

_____ 6. How did Bertram react to the forced and uneasy marriage commanded by the king?
    a) He went home to his mother alone.
    b) He desired Helena to apply to the king for him for leave of absence from court.
    c) He and spoke words of rejection and scorn to Helena every day.
    d) He started an affair with Diana.

_____ 7. What object must Helena get to make Bertram approve of her as his wife?
    a) Bertram's portrait.   b) Bertram's attire.
    c) Bertram's ring.   d) Bertram's letter.

_____ 8. How did the king reward Diana for her notable service?
    a) He bestowed upon her a purse of money.
    b) He bestowed upon her precious jewelry.

c) He conferred upon her countess of Capulets.
d) He bestowed upon her a noble husband.

5 Discussions

1. What and how does one's birth influence a person in thoughts and/or actions? How can a person alter his/her future fate—by hardwork, by ability, by intelligence, or by faith? Take Helena as an example.

2. What do you think of the marriage that was endowed by the king of France? Should this power be granted to satisfy Helena's (the king's) will by sacrificing Bertram's objection?

3. How could Bertram believe that he spent the night conversing with Diana (but not with Helena)? Couldn't he recognize Diana's figure, her voice, and her gestures, even her reactions to his words? Was love "blind"(and "deaf" in this case?

6 Summary

One of your good friends does not know the story of *All's Well*, use your own words to give him/her a summary of no more than 200 words. Write it below.

_____

_____

_____

_____

_____

_____

_____

7 Character Study

Helena is the central figure in the story, and she is of an extraordinary character.

a. What makes her intelligent, brave and determined?

6

b. Imagine what the complex thoughts were going on in her mind when she heard that:

1) Bertram was leaving for Paris.
2) Bertram would leave her and made her to go to his mother's home.
3) Bertram was wooing Diana.

8 Your Point of View

1. You are King of France. You are terribly ill, but no one can cure you. You cannot afford death because the whole country's social, economic, educational, and cultural affairs, etc. all depend on you. Then, here comes Helena, who is 30 years younger than you and has no experience whatsoever in medical practice, volunteers to cure you. Will you let her try? Why or why not?

2. You are Bertram, born of a noble family and has received very good breeding and education. King of France is now commanding you to marry a lady whom you don't know well, let along love. What would you do? Defend for yourself.

3. You are Diana. You are beautiful and were brought up by a virtuous mother. One day, you met this foreign married man called Bertram. He has fallen in love with you and now comes to you every night, trying to win your love. How would you respond to him?

《終成眷屬》 Answers

2 Vocabulary
A.

1. disposition
2. prevailed
3. hazarded
4. observance
5. cordial
6. discreet

3 Identification
A.

1. Helena
2. the Widow
3. Diana

B.

1. Countess of Rousillon
2. Helena
3. Bertram
4. King of France
5. Lafeu

4 Comprehension

1. b
2. d
3. c
4. a
5. a
6. b
7. c
8. d

《一報還一報》 Practice

1 Postreading

Give your first impressions after reading this story.

2 Vocabulary

1. In the city of Vienna there once reigned a duke of such a mild and gentle temper, that he suffered his subjects to neglect the laws with <u>impunity</u>.

   Impunity means _____

2. This gentleman whom I would save had an honorable father, for whose sake I pray you pardon the young man's <u>transgression</u>.
   Transgression means _____

3. Isabel had that day entered her noviciate in the convent, and it was her intent, after passing through her <u>probation</u> as a novice, to take the veil. **Probation** means _____

4. I'll bribe you with prayers from preserved souls, from fasting maids whose minds are dedicated to nothing <u>temporal</u>.

   Temporal means _____

5. My unsoiled name, the austereness of my life, my word <u>vouched</u> against yours, will outweigh your accusation.
   Vouch means _____

6. The sense of death is most in <u>apprehension</u>, and the poor beetle that we tread upon, feels a pang as great as when a giant dies. **Apprehension** means _____

7. The thoughts of death now overcame the <u>constancy</u> of Claudio's temper, and terrors, such as the guilty only at their deaths do know, <u>assailing</u> him, he cried out: 'Sweet sister, let me live!

   Constancy means _____;

   assail means _____

9

8. His unjust unkindness, that in all reason should have <u>quenched</u> her love, has, like an <u>impediment</u> in the current, made it more unruly.

Quench means _____;

impediment means _____

---

3 **Identification: Fill in the blanks with the characters from the following list.**

Angelo	Claudio	The duke	Escalus
Isabella	Juliet	Mariana	Lucio

A. Who are they?

1. _____ Isabella's school friend, who was led into this transgression by her affection for Claudio.

2. _____ Angelo's wife, who lost her marriage dowry, her brother, and the affections of her husband in the wreck.

3. _____ A novice, who made her petition in the most moving terms for her brother's life and stirred the stern deputy's temper.

4. _____ A gentleman, who had seduced a young lady from her parents and was sentenced to be beheaded.

5. _____ A man, who, bearing the reputation of a saint for his strict and rigid life, was chosen as a fit person to act as the deputy for the duke.

6. _____ A man, who deputed another to the full exercise of his power habited like a friar in his absence.

B. Who said these words?

1. _____ "If any man in Vienna be of worth to undergo such ample grace and honour, it is lord Angelo."

2. _____ "We must not make a scare-crow of the law, setting it up to frighten birds of prey, till custom, finding it harmless, makes it their perch, and not their terror."

3. _____ "Why do you give me this shame? Think you I can fetch a resolution from flowery tenderness? If I must die, I will encounter darkness as a bride, and hug it in my arms."

4. _____ "Our doubts are traitors, and make us lose the good we might often win, by fearing to attempt it."

5. _____ "No ceremony that to great ones belongs, not the king's crown, nor the deputed sword, the marshal's truncheon, nor the judge's robe, becomes them with one half so good a grace as mercy does."

6. _____ "The cunning enemy of mankind, to catch a saint, with saints does bait the hook. Never could an immodest woman once stir my temper, but this virtuous woman subdues me quite."

7. _____ "As there comes light from heaven, and truth from breath, as there is sense in truth and truth in virtue."

8. _____ "Should Isabel kneel down to beg for mercy, her brother's ghost would break his paved bed, and take her hence in horror."

---

4 **Comprehension: Choose the correct answer.**

____ 1. The law that doomed any man who lived with a woman that was not his wife to the punishment of death was never put in force in Vienna. Why?
a) Because of the lenity of the duke.
b) Because the subjects disregarded it on purpose.
c) Because the subjects all lead a strict and rigid life.
d) Because this law was totally forgotten.

____ 2. What did the duke do to put this law in effect?
a) He made a sudden change in himself from the indulgence he had hitherto shown, to the strict severity requisite to check this abuse.
b) He dressed himself as a friar and preached the holy institution of marriage.
c) He married Isabel and used her virtue as the excellent example to work a complete reformation among the young ladies of that city.

    d) He absented himself a while from his dukedom and deputed another to the full exercise of his power.

____ 3. Why did Claudio had great hopes in Isabel's pleading for him?
    a) She will bribe the deputy with golden treasures or glittering stones.
    b) She can discourse with prosperous art, and well she can persuade; besides, there is a speechless dialect in youthful sorrow, such as moves men.
    c) She will sue, kneel, weep, and make men give like gods.
    d) She being a saint, can bait the hook with herself to catch another saint Angelo.

____ 4. On what condition did Angelo promised to give Isabel her brother's life?
    a) That she would give such gifts that Heaven itself would share with him.
    b) That she would teach Claudio the way to heaven, preaching to him the words of penitence.
    c) That she would yield to him her virgin honor and transgress as Juliet had done with Claudio.
    d) That she would lay her life down for Claudios deliverance as frankly as a pin.

____ 5. Why did Claudio pray Isabel to preserve his life by her shame?
    a) He thought of death and terrors.
    b) He thought of his beloved Juliet.
    c) He thought of his perpetual honour.
    d) He thought of his father's voice.

____ 6. In the friar's plan, who would go to the appointment with Angelo at midnight?
    a) The friar.   b) Mariana.   c) Juliet.   d) Isabel.

____ 7. What happened after the secret appointment that night?
    a) Angelo found out that it was Mariana who came to him instead.
    b) Angelo fell in love with Isabel and released Claudio from the prison.

c) Angelo felt all the pangs of the remorse and horror for an intentional crime.

d) Angelo commanded that Claudio should be beheaded, and his head sent to him by five o'clock in the morning.

___ 8. Who was the deputed judge and umpire in Angelo's cause?

a) The duke. b) Escalus. c) Angelo. d) Isabel.

5 Discussions

1. Should the duke, in order not to be regarded as a tyrant, avoid the responsibility for the neglect of the laws among his subjects, which was primarily due to his own indulgence? Discuss the validity of his intent to reform the dishonorable love with his decision to depute Angelo.

2. A hypocrite is one who falsely makes himself appear virtuous or good. Do you consider Angelo a hypocrite? Why? How do you explain Angelo's severity of executing the law? Was it a reflection of his strict and rigid character, or a disapproval of the duke's lenity? Was it out of his respect for the law, or his cruelty to torment Claudio and making him an example for the others? Discuss the difference between justice and cruelty.

6 What Happened?

What do you think happened between Angelo and Mariana that night? Why couldn't he tell that she was not Isabel? Create the scene with your imagination.

7 Change the Law

You're the duke. After the case of Claudio was closed, you realized that the law was too harsh and decided to revise it. How would you change it? Make the punishment appropriate according to different cases and their variations.

8 Organize a Talk Show

You are a host/hostess of a program that discusses controversial issues. You would like to talk about the events of Measure for Measure in your show.

1. What issues would you bring up?
2. Who would you like to invite to your show as the guests?
3. What possible questions would you ask them to comment on?

9 Contemporary Point of View

If Measure for Measure happened in the 21th Century, would the thoughts, actions, and decisions remain the same as in the story we're just read? Speak from your point of view.

1. You were in Isabel, would you yield to Angelo in order to save your brother? Would you marry the duke?
2. You were Claudio, would you ask your sister to sacrifice her honour to keep your life?
3. You were Angelo, would you put Claudio to death? Would you threaten Isabel with your political power?
4. You were Mariana, would you accept Angelo as your husband after he abandoned you? Would you help the duke/friar with his scheme?

《一報還一報》 Answers

3 Identification

A.

1. Juliet
2. Mariana
3. Isabella
4. Claudio
5. Angelo
6. the duke

B.

1. Escalus
2. Angelo
3. Claudio
4. Lucio
5. Isabella
6. Angelo
7. Mariana
8. the duke

4 Comprehension

1. a
2. d
3. b
4. c
5. a
6. b
7. d
8. c

《終成眷屬》中譯

P.26 父親剛過世，盧西昂伯爵貝特漢繼承爵位和財產。法王很喜愛貝特漢的父親，他一聽到這個死訊，就派人去召他兒子立刻前來巴黎王宮。念在和已故伯爵的一場交情上，法王打算特別照顧抬舉年輕的貝特漢。

法國宮廷的老臣拉福要來帶貝特漢去見國王時，貝特漢和寡母伯爵夫人住在一起。法王是個專制的君主，他用下諭旨或下令的方式請人去宮裡，任再顯貴的臣民，也無法抗旨。因此，剛喪夫的伯爵夫人要和心愛的兒子分離，儘管宛如再度痛失丈夫，她仍不敢多留兒子一天，立刻囑咐他上路。

P.27 伯爵夫人死了丈夫，兒子又突然要離開，前來接兒子的拉福試圖安慰她。他用朝臣的那種客氣態度說，國王是個仁厚君主，會待她宛若夫君，待她兒子宛若人父。這意思是說，好心的國王會提攜貝特漢。

拉福還告訴伯爵夫人，國王染了重病，御醫已經宣佈無藥可救。聽到國王的病況，夫人表示十分難過。她說，但願海倫娜（在場服侍她的一位小姑娘）的父親還在人世，因為她相信海倫娜的父親一定能夠治好國王陛下的病。

P.28 她跟拉福提了一下海倫娜的身世。她說，海倫娜是名醫賈合・德・柯柏的獨生女，他臨死前把女兒託付給她照顧，因此自從他死了之後，她就一直帶著海倫娜。伯爵夫人接著稱讚海倫娜本性賢慧，品德高尚，說她這些美德都承自了她那可敬的父親。

當她說這些話時，海倫娜不發一聲，逕自傷心地哭了起來。伯爵夫人見狀，便溫和地數落她不該為父親的死太過悲傷。

貝特漢向母親道別。伯爵夫人含淚辭別，一再祝福寶貝兒子，並把他託付給拉福。她說道：「我的好大人，您要多指點他，他還是個不曉人事的臣子呀。」

P.29 貝特漢最後跟海倫娜說了幾句話，但只是出於禮貌，祝福她快樂。對這段短短的臨別前言，他結尾說：「善待我的母親，好好侍候妳這女主人。」

海倫娜心儀貝特漢已久，事實上當她不發一聲地傷心哭泣時，那淚水並不是為了賈合・德・柯柏而流的。她愛父親，但此時此刻，她對貝特漢的情意更深，卻眼見即將要失去他。她已經忘記死去父親的樣子和容貌，現在除了貝特漢，她心裡頭什麼人的影子也沒有。

雖然她老早就愛上了貝特漢，但她不曾忘記他是盧西昂伯爵，是法國最古老家族的後裔，而她卻出身低微，父母名不見經傳。貝特漢的祖先都是貴族，所以她把出身高貴的貝特漢當作是主人，是她親愛的少爺。除了終身服侍他，做一輩子的家僕，她不敢有任何奢望。

P.31 他地位尊貴，她出身低下，兩人身世懸殊。她常說：「我愛上一顆閃耀明星，還想和星星結婚。貝特漢太高不可攀了。」

貝特漢離開了。她淚眼婆娑，傷心不已。她愛他，但不認為兩人有希望，能夠時時刻刻看到他，她已經心滿意足了。她會坐下來，仰望他的深色眼眸、彎彎眉毛和柔軟的鬍髮，直到彷彿能在心版上畫出他的肖像。那心愛臉龐上的每一個線條，她都牢記在心裡。

賈吉‧德‧柄柏過世後沒有留下遺產，只留了一些良帖秘方給她。他深入研究和長期經驗的累積，得到了這些高明幾乎萬能丹的藥方。

P.32 拉福說，國王害了病，日漸虛弱，而其中正好有個處方寫明可以醫治。一聽說國王龍體不適，海倫娜雖仍不免覺得自己出身卑微，希望渺茫，但她心下還是起了個雄心計畫，打算隻身前往巴黎，救治國王。

海倫娜手裡是握有這箋祕方，但國王和御醫既已認定無藥可救，因此即使她請求醫治，諒他們也不見得會相信一個無學無知的姑娘。但她堅信，只要獲准一試，成功的把握可能還會比父親醫術所能保證的來得更大，即使父親生前是最聞名的大夫。她感受到一股強大的信念，覺得這帖良藥蒙受天上一切吉星之眷顧，是一份足以改善她命運的遺產，甚至可以使她高攀成為盧西昂伯爵夫人。

P.33 貝特漢離開不久，管家就通報伯爵夫人說，他無意中聽到海倫娜在自言自語，從她的隻字片語中，知道她愛上了貝特漢，想跟他到巴黎去。伯爵夫人謝過管家，要他下去，並通知海倫娜過來，她有話要跟她說。

聽到海倫娜的事，伯爵夫人不禁往事湧上心頭。那時，約莫是她初愛上貝特漢的父親之際，她自言自語說：「我年輕時也是這個樣子的。愛情，是青春玫瑰上的一根刺。我們是自然之子，青春時代時不免犯了這些錯，儘管當時並不以為有錯。」

伯爵夫人正沈思自己青春時代所犯的愛情過錯時，海倫娜走了進來。

P.34 夫人對她說：「海倫娜，妳知道我就像是妳的母親。」

海倫娜回答：「您是我尊貴的女主人。」

伯爵夫人再度強調：「妳是我的女兒，為什麼一聽我說我是妳的母親，妳就臉色蒼白？」

海倫娜擔心夫人瞧出她的心思，所以一臉驚惶，思緒慌亂。她依舊回答：「夫人，請原諒我呀，您並不是我的母親，盧西昂伯爵不可能是我哥哥，我也不是您的女兒啊。」

伯爵夫人說：「可是海倫娜，妳可以做我的兒媳婦啊。我想妳是有此意，所以『母親』和『女兒』這兩個詞才讓妳不安。海倫娜，妳愛不愛我兒子？」

「好心的夫人，您原諒我呀。」驚慌的海倫娜說道。

伯爵夫人又問了一次同樣的問題：「妳愛不愛我兒子嗎？」

「您不也愛他嗎，夫人？」海倫娜說。

伯爵夫人回答：「海倫娜，妳答話不要閃爍其詞。來吧，把妳的心意講出來，大家都看得出來妳的愛意了。」

P.36 海倫娜跪了下來，坦承自己的感情，又羞又驚地乞求這個貴族女主人原諒她。她表示自己知道兩人門不當戶不對，並表示貝特漢不知道她的情意。她把她卑微無望的愛比喻成一個可憐的印地安人：印地安人崇拜太陽，太陽雖然也照耀著這位崇拜者，可是卻不知道他究竟是何人。

17

伯爵夫人問海倫娜最近是否想去巴黎。她坦承，當她聽到拉福提到國王的病時，心裡頭的確起了這個念頭。

「這是妳想去巴黎的動機嗎？」伯爵夫人説：「是嗎？妳老實説。」

海倫娜老實答道：「是少爺讓我起了這個念頭的，要不然，什麼巴黎、藥方或國王，我當時都不想。」

聽了這番完整的告白，伯爵夫人沒説半句贊成或是責怪的話，只是認真盤問海倫娜那帖藥方是否真有可能救治國王。

P.37 伯爵夫人發現，那是賈合‧德‧栁柏所有藥方中最珍貴的一箋，他在臨死之前才傳給女兒。她又想起那可怕的一刻，她正式答應過要照顧這姑娘。如今，這位姑娘的命運和國王的性命，似乎都要看這計畫能否實現了（計畫雖是出自一位痴情姑娘的痴心想法，但伯爵夫人心想那或許是天意，冥冥之中要醫治好國王，也讓賈合‧德‧栁柏之女的未來命運有個好基礎）。於是她准許海倫娜完全按自己的意思進行，又慷慨資助她充分的盤纏，並派了些合適的隨從跟去。帶著伯爵夫人的祝福，以及盼望她成功的好心祈願，海倫娜隨即往巴黎而去。

P.39 海倫娜抵達巴黎後，靠老臣子拉福這位友人的幫忙，她獲准晉見國王。但她還得面臨許多難關，因為要勸國王試服這位美麗年輕的大夫所獻的藥方，並非易事。她告訴國王，自己是賈合‧德‧栁柏的女兒（國王早聞其大名），而她所獻的珍貴藥方，宛如珍寶，集父親長期經驗和醫術之精華。她還大膽承諾，若兩天之內，不能使陛下完全恢復健康，那她甘受死罪。

國王最後答應一試。兩天之內，國王若無法病癒，海倫娜就得受死；然而要是她成功了，國王答應任由她在全法國的男子之中（除了王子之外），挑選中意的人來做丈夫。要是她能治好國王的病，她所要求的報酬就是任她挑選自己的丈夫。

P.41 海倫娜料想得沒錯，父親的藥方果然奏效，沒讓她希望落空。不出兩天，國王就完全恢復了健康。他召集宮中所有年輕的貴族，以便依約報償，賜給美麗大夫一位新郎。他要海倫娜瞧瞧這群年輕的單身貴族，挑一個來做丈夫。

海倫娜很快做好選擇，因為她在這群年輕的臣子當中瞥見了盧西昂伯爵。她轉向貝特漢，説道：「就是這一位了。少爺，我不敢説我挑中了您，但只要我在世，蒙您指導，我就把自己獻給您，為您服務。」

國王説：「啊，那麼，年輕的貝特漢，把她帶回去吧，她是你的妻子了。」

貝特漢毫不遲疑地公然表示：他不喜歡國王這個自己送上門來的禮物。他説，海倫娜是個窮大夫的女兒，她從前在她父親的照料下長大，現在則靠他母親的施惠過活。

P.42 聽到他説這些拒絕的輕蔑話，海倫娜對國王説：「陛下，見您康復，草民甚喜，其他的就作罷吧。」

但國王容不得他的諭旨被藐視，賜與貴族婚姻可是法王的眾多特權之一。於是，貝特漢只好當天娶下海倫娜。對貝特漢而言，這是一樁不稱心的逼婚，對那位可憐的姑娘來說，也沒有遠景可言。她冒著生命的危險，得到這個貴族丈夫，可是贏來的似乎只是一場空歡喜，因為丈夫的心並不是法王權力所能賜與的禮物。

一結完婚，貝特漢就要海倫娜代他向國王請求，答應讓他離開宮廷。當她告知國王已批准他離開時，貝特漢告訴她，對於這場突如其來的婚姻，他毫無準備，十分苦惱，因此對於他下一步的打算，她也不需要感到驚訝。

就算她不驚訝，但發現他有意要離開她，她也不免傷心。

P.44 他命令她回到他母親的家。聽到他這無情的話，海倫娜說道：「先生，這件事我無話可說。我的出身不起眼，不配享有這種福氣，但我是你最順從的僕人，絕對會真心侍奉您，好彌補這種缺憾。」

海倫娜這番謙卑的說辭，絲毫也不能打動高傲的貝特漢，讓他憐惜這溫柔的妻子。他甚至連親切道別時的客套話也沒說，就離開了她。

海倫娜只好回到伯爵夫人的身邊。她完成了這趟旅程的目的，既救了國王一命，也和心愛的少爺盧西昂伯爵成了親。然而當她沮喪地回到貴族婆婆那裡時，才一進家門，就收到貝特漢的一封信，幾乎教她斷腸。

P.46 好心的伯爵夫人熱忱接待她，當她是兒子親自挑選的妻子，視她是出身高貴的婦人。見貝特漢惡意冷落，新婚之日就打發她一人獨自回家，伯爵夫人說了些好話來安慰她。

但親切的接待並不能排解海倫娜心裡的悲傷。她說：「夫人，我丈夫走了，永遠不會回來了。」

她讀著貝特漢的信：

> 等妳拿到我手上這枚永遠也不會拿下來的戒指時，再叫我丈夫吧，但是「永遠」都不會有「那一刻」的。

P.47 「這真是可怕的宣判！」海倫娜說。

伯爵夫人請她耐下性子，說貝特漢現在是走了，但她是她的孩子了，理當是個貴族，受得起讓二十個像貝特漢這種粗魯男孩來服侍她，終日稱她是夫人。可是無論這位仁厚無比的婆婆如何恭敬地屈尊，如何好心地說好話，都無法撫慰兒媳婦的悲傷。

海倫娜的眼睛直盯著信看，傷心欲絕地哭喊道：

> 法國讓我無所留戀，
> 除非我在法國沒有妻子。

伯爵夫人問她：這句話是否是信裡所寫的？

「正是啊，夫人。」可憐的海倫娜只能這樣回答。

P.48 第二天早上，海倫娜失蹤了。她走後留下一封信給伯爵夫人，向她說明自己突然離去的緣由。她在信裡說道，她逼得貝特漢離開故鄉家園，心中萬分難過。為了彌補過失，她要前往聖佳克‧勒‧葛洪聖壇朝聖。最後，她請伯爵夫人通知她兒子，說他痛恨的妻子已經永遠離開他的家園了。

離開巴黎後，貝特漢來到佛羅倫斯，在佛羅倫斯公爵的軍隊裡頭當軍官。一場勝役後，他因作戰驍勇，顯赫一時。之後他收到母親的來信，得知海倫娜不再糾纏他的好消息。

就在他準備啟程返家時，穿著朝聖裝的海倫娜也來到了佛羅倫斯城。

P.49 在以前，佛羅倫斯是朝聖者前往聖佳克‧勒‧葛洪的必經城市。海倫娜來到這個城市之後，聽說當地有一個殷勤好客的寡婦，時常在家裡接待前往那位聖徒神廟的女朝聖者，除了親切款待，並供給住宿。海倫娜跑去找這位善心女士，寡婦殷勤地招呼她，邀請她去參觀這座名城的各種新奇事物，還問她是否想瞧瞧公爵的軍隊，她可以帶她去視野廣闊的地方看看。

「而且妳還會看到貴國的同胞。」寡婦說：「他叫盧西昂伯爵，在公爵的戰役中建功立勳。」

一聽到能夠看到貝特漢，海倫娜不需寡婦再三邀請，就答應前去。她隨女東道主一道走，想到能再見親愛丈夫的臉，那種喜悅真是既傷心又悲涼。

「這男人長得很俊秀吧？」寡婦說。

「我很喜歡他。」海倫娜由衷地回答。

P.51 她們沿途走著，健談的寡婦一路上談的都是貝特漢。她把貝特漢的婚姻經過告訴海倫娜，說他如何遺棄那個嫁給他的可憐婦人，為了不和她住在一起，還跑來加入公爵的軍隊。

海倫娜耐心聽著自己不幸的遭遇，但說完了這些，貝特漢的故事卻還沒結束。寡婦接下來又講起另一個故事。這故事的字字句句都刺痛海倫娜的心，因為寡婦說的是貝特漢如何迷戀她女兒。

貝特漢是不喜歡國王逼他成親，但他看起來也不是個不懂愛情的人。他隨軍隊駐紮佛羅倫斯時，愛上了年輕貌美的淑女黛安娜，也就是這位接待海倫娜的寡婦之女。每晚，他都會來黛安娜的窗下追求她，彈奏各種音樂，高唱歌曲，歌頌她的美貌。他所請求的，無非不是要黛安娜允許他在她家人都歇息之後，偷偷去和她相會。

P.53 可是黛安娜知道他是已婚男子，所以無論如何也不為所動，既不肯答應這個不成體統的要求，也不回應他的追求。黛安娜是在嚴母的教導下長大的，雖然寡婦現在家道中落，但也是系出名門，為開普雷世家的後代。

好心的夫人把這些都告訴了海倫娜，她大大誇獎她這謹慎的女兒恪守禮教，又說這完全要歸功於她給她的良好教育和教誨。她又說，貝特漢最近特別糾纏不清，期待黛安娜今晚首肯一見，因為他隔天一早就要離開佛羅倫斯了。

聽到貝特漢愛上寡婦的女兒，海倫娜很難過。但又聽她這麼一說，海倫娜急中生智，計畫找回逃婚的丈夫。（雖然上次的計畫失敗，但她並不氣餒）

P.54 她向寡婦表白自己就是貝特漢的棄婦海倫娜。她請求好心的女東道主和她的女兒這次能接受貝特漢的來訪，並允許她代替黛安娜和貝特漢相會。她告訴她們，她這次想和丈夫偷偷相會，主要是為了拿到他的戒指。丈夫曾說過，只要她拿到那枚戒指，他就承認她是他的妻子。

寡婦和她的女兒很同情這個不幸的棄婦，再加上海倫娜答應酬謝她們，讓她們很心動，便答應相助此事。海倫娜先給她們一袋錢，作為日後酬謝的定金。

當天，海倫娜要人送消息給貝特漢，說她已經去世。希望他聽到她的死訊後，認為自己有權可以再物色他人，然後向假扮黛安娜的海倫娜求婚。只要能夠得到戒指和結婚諾言，她相信自己就能讓這件事有好的結果。

P.56 傍晚天黑之後，貝特漢獲准進入黛安娜的繡房，而海倫娜早就在裡頭準備好接待他了。

他對海倫娜傾吐纏綿情話，儘管她心裡明白這些話是說給黛安娜聽的，但仍覺得珍貴。貝特漢非常迷戀她，鄭重承諾要做她的丈夫，永遠愛她。要是他知道了說著讓他興奮不已的話的人，正是他鄙視的妻子海倫娜，海倫娜希望今晚的諾言，會是真正愛情的兆頭。

貝特漢從來沒發現過海倫娜是個聰明的姑娘，要不然，他可能就不會那樣看不上她了。再加上兩人天天相見，他也就完全沒注意到她的美麗。要是習慣常常見到某人的臉孔，就無法像第一眼見到時那樣，留下深刻的美醜印象。另外，貝特漢也無法感受到海倫娜的善解人意，她對他如此又敬又愛，所以她在他面前時總是一語不發。

P.58 可現在，她日後的命運和她的愛情計畫是否皆能圓滿落幕，都得看她今晚相會時能否在貝特漢的心中留下美好印象，於是她竭盡所能來討他歡心。她言談活潑，坦率又通情達理，態度可愛又甜美，讓貝特漢傾心不已，貝特漢於是宣誓娶她為妻。

P.59 海倫娜要他脫下戒指，做為定情之物，他於是交上戒指。對她來說，擁有這枚戒指很重要，而她則把國王御賜的戒指拿給他，以做為交換。

早晨天色未明之際，她送走貝特漢，貝特漢立刻啟程返回母親家。

海倫娜說服寡婦和黛安娜跟她一道回巴黎。為完全實現她的計畫，她需要她們進一步的支援。她們抵達巴黎時，發現國王已去拜訪盧西昂伯爵夫人，海倫娜於是盡全力欲趕上國王。

國王龍體已經大安，但仍滿心感激海倫娜救了他。他一見到盧西昂伯爵夫人，就聊起海倫娜，說海倫娜是她兒子因為愚蠢而失去的一顆珍貴寶石。伯爵夫人為海倫娜的死正傷慟不已，國王看到自己的話又讓她傷心，只好說道：「我的好夫人，這一切我都已經原諒了，也已經忘了。」

P.61 本性善良的老拉福也在場，他無法忍受他心疼的海倫娜這樣被人輕易遺忘。他說：「這臣非說不可了，這個年輕的臣子對他的國王陛下、母親和妻子，都太不知分寸了。不過他最對不起的還是他自己，因為他失去了一個令人驚艷的美麗妻子，而且她說話讓人信服，十全十美，任誰都想服侍她。」

國王表示：「讚美逝者，愈添美好回憶。這樣吧，把他叫過來。」國王指的是貝特漢，現在他人就在國王面前。他對自己傷害海倫娜的事，深表歉意。看在他的亡父和可敬母親的份上，國王饒恕了他，回復對他的寵幸。

P.62 未料，國王的慈顏卻突然對他愀然變色，原來，國王看到他手上戴著自己御賜給海倫娜的戒指。國王記得一清二楚，海倫娜曾對著所有聖徒立誓，永遠不讓戒指離手，當她遭遇重大變故時，才會把戒指送還給國王本人。國王追問他戒指是哪兒來的，貝特漢編了個不可信的謊，說是一位姑娘從窗台上丟給他的，並且表示他從結婚那天以後，就沒再見過海倫娜。

P.64 國王知道貝特漢不中意妻子，恐將她殺害，便下令侍衛捉拿貝特漢，說道：「我腦裡縈繞著一種可怕的想法，我怕海倫娜已經慘遭謀殺了。」

這時，黛安娜和母親走進來，向國王請願，請求陛下運用王權強迫貝特漢娶黛安娜，因為他已對她立過正式的婚約宣誓。貝特漢深怕國王生氣，連忙否認他宣誓過。黛安娜於是取出戒指（海倫娜把它交到她手裡的），證實自己所言不假。她表示，他發誓娶她時，為了還禮，她就把貝特漢現在所戴著的戒指送給他。

一聽到這裡，國王命令侍衛也將她捉拿。她和貝特漢兩人對戒指的說辭不一樣，更加確認國王所疑有據。國王表示，要是他們不招供海倫娜的戒指從何得來，兩人就要一併處斬。

P.66 黛安娜請求讓她母親去把那個賣戒指給她的珠寶商帶來，國王批准。寡婦離開不久，就帶著海倫娜本人回來。

看到兒子處境危險，好伯爵夫人默默地兀自傷悲，也很害怕兒子殺妻的嫌疑會是真的。如今看到她曾視如己出的親愛的海倫娜還活著，她欣喜欲狂。國王同樣也喜出望外，不敢相信那人就是海倫娜，他說：「我看到的這個人真的就是貝特漢的妻子嗎？」

海倫娜自覺妻子的身分尚未獲得承認，就答道：「不，好陛下，您看到的只是一個妻子的影子罷了，有名無實。」

貝特漢大喊：「有名有實！有名有實！啊，原諒我吧！」

海倫娜表示：「喔，少爺，我扮成這位美麗姑娘時，發現你非常體貼。你看，這是你寫的信！」她用愉快的語調，把她一度傷心反覆唸過的話讀給他聽：等妳拿到我手上這只永遠也不會拿下來的戒指時，……「我辦到了，你把戒指給了我。如今我贏得你兩次了，你願意做我的丈夫嗎？」

P.67 貝特漢回答：「只要妳能證明那天晚上和我談話的女子就是妳，那我就會永遠好好地愛妳。」

這並不難，因為寡婦和黛安娜隨海倫娜一道來，正是為了證明這件事實。海倫娜效勞過國王，國王很看重她，又因黛安娜好心幫助海倫娜，於是國王也很喜歡黛安娜。為此，國王也許了黛安娜一位貴族丈夫。海倫娜的事給了國王一個啟示：美麗姑娘要是有了特別的功勞，國王最佳的賞賜就是賜給她們丈夫。

就這樣，海倫娜終於知道，父親留下的遺產果然蒙受天上一切吉星之眷顧。如今，她是親愛的貝特漢所鍾愛的妻子，是貴族夫人的兒媳婦，而她自己也貴為盧西昂伯爵夫人了。

P.84 一位性情溫和寬宏的公爵曾經治理過維也納城,他對人民從不施懲行罰。特別是有一條法律,因公爵在位期間還未曾執行過,所以幾乎被人遺忘。

這條法律規定,凡與妻子以外的婦女同居,一律處死。因公爵寬大,這條法律完全受到漠視,神聖的婚姻制度不被重視,天天可見有年輕女兒的維也納父母跑來見公爵,投訴他們照顧的女兒被勾引,跑去和單身男子同居。

看到民間這種不良風氣愈來愈熾盛,好心的公爵很難過。但他想,自己向來為政寬厚,若為了匡正惡習,突然變得嚴律苛政,人民(一向擁戴他)必定會把他當成暴君。

P.85 為此,他決定暫時離開公國,由代理人全權掌政。如此一來,既可行法禁止不當的戀愛行為,自己也不用因為變得嚴苛而招致民怨。

公爵選了安哲羅來擔當此項重責大任。安哲羅是個因生活嚴謹而在維也納享有聖徒之譽的人,公爵認為他是最佳人選。公爵跟御前參事艾斯卡大臣透露此計,艾斯卡表示:「在維也納城,能配享此一隆恩光榮者,就屬安哲羅大人了。」

P.86 公爵托言去波蘭。他離開維也納,告假期間由安哲羅擔任攝政。事實上公爵出城只是個晃子,他悄悄返回維也納,喬裝成修士,打算暗中觀察這看似聖人的安哲羅的作為。

就在安哲羅受命就任新職後不久,有位叫做克勞狄的紳士,將一位年輕姑娘從她父母身邊誘拐走。對於這宗罪行,新任攝政下令,將克勞狄收押並打入牢裡。安哲羅根據這條被忽視已久的舊有法律,判克勞狄斬首處決。

請求寬恕年輕克勞狄的聲浪高漲,連好心的老臣艾斯卡本人也為他說項:「哎呀!我想搭救的這位先生有個德高望重的父親,看在他父親的份上,請求您寬恕這年輕人的罪吧。」

P.87 安哲羅回答:「法律不能像稻草人一樣,豎立起來只能嚇唬嚇唬來捕食的鳥。鳥習慣之後,見稻草人傷不了自己,不但不再怕它,還會在上頭棲息。大人,他非死不可。」

好友陸西歐去監獄探視克勞狄。克勞狄對他說:「拜託你,陸西歐,幫我個忙,去找我姐姐伊莎貝拉,她今天就要進里克雷修道院了。請告訴她我情況危急,求她去和嚴苛的攝政說說情,親自去見安哲羅一趟。她辯才無礙,善於勸說,而且她少女的憂鬱中有某種難喻的特質,足以打動男人,我想這樣成功的希望會很大。」

23

P.88 正如克勞狄所説，姐姐伊莎貝拉當天進入修道院見習，準備在通過修女的見習期後，正式成為修女。正當她向一位修女詢問修道院的清規時，她們聽到了陸西歐的聲音。陸西歐走進修道院，説道：「願主賜與此地平安！」

「是誰在説話？」伊莎貝拉説。

「是男人的聲音。」修女答道：「好伊莎貝拉，妳去看看，問他有何貴事。妳可以去，我不行。成為修女之後，除了當著修道院長的面，不可以和任何異性説話，而且説話時也不能露出自己的臉，如果露出臉，就不可以説話。」

「妳們修女還有其他權利嗎？」伊莎貝拉問。

「這些還不夠嗎？」修女回答。

「不，夠了。」伊莎貝拉説：「我這麼問並不是想要更多的權利，而是希望侍奉聖克雷的姊妹們能持更嚴格的清規。」

P.89 她們又聽到陸西歐的聲音。修女説：「他又在叫了，請妳去招呼他吧。」

伊莎貝拉走出去見陸西歐，向他回禮致意，説道：「平安豐足！是誰在説話？」

陸西歐恭敬地走向她，説道：「這位童貞女，天佑妳。妳臉頰紅潤，應當就是一位童貞女吧！能請妳帶我去見伊莎貝拉嗎？她是這裡的見習修女，也是一位不幸兄弟克勞狄的美麗姐姐。」

「請問，為什麼説是不幸的兄弟？」伊莎貝拉説：「我就是他的姐姐伊莎貝拉。」

「美麗溫柔的小姐。」他回答：「妳弟弟要我好好問候妳，他坐牢了。」

「哎呀！怎麼回事啊？」伊莎貝拉問。

P.90 陸西歐告訴她，克勞狄因為勾引一位少女，身繫囹圄。

她説：「噯，該不會是表妹茱麗葉吧。」

茱麗葉和伊莎貝拉並非親戚，但為紀念兩人在學校時的情誼，便互稱表姊妹。伊莎貝拉知道茱麗葉迷戀克勞狄，擔心她會因愛戀他而犯法。

「正是她。」陸西歐回答。

「那就讓我弟弟娶茱麗葉呀。」伊莎貝拉説。

陸西歐表示，克勞狄是很樂意娶茱麗葉，但因他違法，攝政將他判了死刑。他説：「這下只能靠妳了，用好話去説動安哲羅。妳不幸的弟弟要我來找妳，正為此事。」

伊莎貝拉説：「唉！我有什麼能耐幫他？我想我沒有辦法讓安哲羅改變心意的呀。」

24

「疑惑足以敗事呀。」陸西歐說:「害怕嘗試,讓我們錯失可能成功的機會。去找安哲羅大人吧!姑娘們只要跪下來求求情,流流眼淚,男人就會像上帝一樣慷慨大方了。」

P.91 「我試試看好了。」伊莎貝拉說:「我先留下來跟院長報告這件事,然後再去找安哲羅。代我轉告我弟弟,能不能成功,我今晚就會給他消息。」

伊莎貝拉趕去宮廷,跪在安哲羅的面前說:「大人啊,我是個苦命人,請大人聽我申訴呀。」

「妳有什麼要申訴的?」安哲羅問。

她於是用最動人的話,乞求讓弟弟免於一死。

安哲羅說:「姑娘啊,這事沒有挽回的餘地了呀,令弟已經定罪,是非死不可了。」

「啊,律法公正,只是太苛!」伊莎貝拉說:「這麼說來,我『曾經有過』弟弟。上帝祝福您!」說罷就準備離開。

P.92 陪她前來的陸西歐說道:「別輕言放棄啊。再回去哀求他,跪在他面前,抓住他的袍子。妳的態度太冷淡了,就算是討一根針,也得說得懇切些才行啊。」

於是伊莎貝拉再度下跪請求開恩。

安哲羅說:「已經定罪了,太遲了。」

「太遲!」伊莎貝拉說:「不,不遲!出口的話可以收回。大人,請您相信,大人物的任何儀仗,舉凡是國王的皇冠、攝政的寶劍、元帥的權杖,或是法官的長袍,比起仁慈所能彰顯的偉大,都還不及一半。」

「請妳走吧。」安哲羅說。

但伊莎貝拉仍向他懇求,她說:「如果把我弟弟換作是您,把您換作是他,您也可能犯同樣的錯,可是他就不會像您這樣嚴厲。但願我有您的權力,而您變成是伊莎貝拉,那我會這樣對待您嗎?不會的。我要讓您了解做法官的滋味,也要讓您了解做犯人又是什麼滋味。」

P.94 「夠了,好姑娘!」安哲羅說:「定妳弟弟罪的是法律,不是我。就算他是我的親戚、手足或兒子,法律還是會這樣定他罪,他明天非死不可了。」

「明天?」伊莎貝拉說:「啊!這太突然了,饒了他,饒了他吧,他還沒有準備好就死。我們就是在廚房裡宰殺雞鴨,也有個季節時令,對獻給上天的東西,難道比對餵飽我們這賤命的食物還草率嗎?好心的大人呀,您想想,犯此罪者何其多,就從未有人因為做我弟弟所做之事而斷送性命的啊。您是第一個定這種罪的人,他是第一個遭受這種刑罰的人。大人啊,請您摸著良心,捫心自問知不知道我弟弟犯的是什麼罪,要是您的良心承認自己也有犯這種罪的本能,那就不要有判我弟弟死罪的想法啊!」

P.95 她最後所説的這些話，比之前所説的更加動搖了安哲羅，因為伊莎貝拉的美貌讓他心下起了邪念。就像克勞狄所犯的罪一樣，他開始有了不正當愛情的念頭。這些內心的衝突使他別過臉，轉身離開伊莎貝拉。伊莎貝拉把他叫回來，説道：「仁慈的大人啊，請您回過身來，聽聽我怎麼賄賂你，好心的大人啊，請轉過身來吧！」

「什麼，賄賂我！」安哲羅説。他很訝異她竟想賄賂他。

「對啊。」伊莎貝拉説：「用連上帝也會與你分享的禮物賄賂你。不是用金銀財寶，也不是用全憑人類喜好而決定價值的閃亮寶石，而是用在日出之前就能傳達到天堂的虔誠祈禱──由無瑕的靈魂、全心奉獻給上帝的齋戒女子所祈禱的。」

P.96 「好吧，妳明天再來找我。」安哲羅説。

弟弟暫時得到緩刑，伊莎貝拉獲准再度上訴，她離開攝政時滿懷喜悦，希望最後能夠改變攝政嚴苛的個性。她臨走時，説道：「願上帝保佑大人平安！願上帝拯救大人！」

安哲羅聽到，就在心裡説道：「阿門！願上帝保佑我不要被妳和妳的美德所惑。」緊接著，他被自己的這些邪念嚇到，説道：「怎麼回事？怎麼回事？我愛上她了嗎？竟想再聽到她説話，想要盯著她的眼睛看？我在痴想什麼呀！人類那狡獪的敵人為了讓聖徒上鉤，就用聖徒來當釣餌。我從沒對放蕩的婦人動心過，可是這個貞潔的女子卻把我治得服服貼貼。即使是現在，男子痴戀女子時，我都還笑他們，覺得他們莫名其妙。」

P.97 當天晚上，安哲羅內心掙扎，充滿罪惡感，比那個被他判了死刑的犯人還難受，因為穿著修士服的好公爵去了牢裡探視克勞狄。公爵指點這個年輕人通往天堂的路，告訴他如何懺悔和祈求平安。

要不要做壞事，安哲羅搖擺不定，甚感痛苦。他一下子想誘惑伊莎貝拉遠離清白貞潔的修道，一下子又為自己的犯罪念頭感到悔恨惶恐。最後，壞念頭佔了上風。這個之前還為賄賂行為大吃一驚的人，如今決定對這位少女大大行賄一番，甚至可以用她親愛弟弟的性命來做為珍貴賄禮，讓她拒絕不了。

P.98 早上，伊莎貝拉前來，安哲羅要她單獨進來見他。進來之後，他對她説，如果她願意把她的初夜獻給他，和他做茱麗葉與克勞狄違法所做的那般事，那他就可以饒她弟弟一命。

他説：「因為，伊莎貝拉，我愛妳。」

伊莎貝拉説：「我弟弟也愛茱麗葉，你説他得為此送上性命。」

安哲羅説：「克勞狄不該死了，只要你答應晚上偷偷跑來找我，就像茱麗葉半夜蹺家去找克勞狄一樣。」

他的話讓伊莎貝拉很吃驚，他定她弟弟的罪，卻又引誘她去犯相同的罪。她説：「為了我不幸的弟弟，也為了我自己，也就是説，若我被判了死刑，我會把身上的一條條鞭痕，當作是穿戴了紅色寶石，像走向我渴望躺上去的床一樣地走向死亡，也不會讓自己蒙受這種恥辱。」她還説，但願他説這些話只是為了考驗她的貞節。

P.100 他説：「相信我，我以人格擔保，我所説的都是我的本意。」

聽到他用「人格」這兩個字來表示這麼齷齪的念頭，伊莎貝拉很惱怒，説道：「哈！你這麼居心不良，有多少人格可以相信呀！安哲羅，我要舉發你，你等著吧！你要不現在就簽一張赦免我弟弟的命令，要不我就到處大聲張揚你是一個什麼樣的人！」

「伊莎貝拉，誰會相信妳？」安哲羅説：「我名聲毫無污點，生活一絲不苟，我那反駁妳的話，遠比妳那控訴我的話更有份量。好好為令弟著想，答應我的要求吧，不然他明天就得死了。至於妳，隨妳怎麼説吧，我的謊言是比妳的實話更有份量的。妳明天就給我個答案吧。」

P.101 「我該向誰喊冤啊？就算我説了，又有誰會相信我？」伊莎貝拉説著，一面走向弟弟被囚禁的陰暗地牢。她到地牢時，弟弟正和公爵談論著神。穿著修士服的公爵也探訪過茱麗葉，讓這對犯罪的戀人清楚自己所犯的過錯。痛苦的茱麗葉流著淚，真心懺悔，告白自己比克勞狄更應該受到責罰，因為是自己心甘情願同意了他那不正當的請求。

伊莎貝拉走進克勞狄被囚禁的牢房，一面説：「願主賜與此地平安、恩典和良伴！」

「是誰？」喬裝過的公爵説：「進來吧，這種祝福受人歡迎。」

P.102 「我來跟克勞狄説一兩句話。」伊莎貝拉説。

公爵留下他們兩人，要看守犯人的獄吏帶他到一個可以偷聽到他們講話的地方。

「姐姐，現在有什麼好消息嗎？」克勞狄問。

伊莎貝拉告訴他得準備明天受死。

「沒有挽救的餘地了嗎？」克勞狄問。

「有啊，弟弟。」伊莎貝拉回答：「是有一個，不過要是你同意了，那你就會名譽掃地，無臉見人。」

「告訴我怎麼回事。」克勞狄説。

「哦，克勞狄，我真替你擔心！」姐姐回答：「我很害怕你貪生，把多個短短六、七寒暑的壽命看得比一生的名譽還重要。你勇於面對死亡嗎？死亡大都是想像時覺得可怕，踩在我們腳下的可憐甲蟲，牠們死時和巨人死時一樣痛苦。」

P.104 「妳為什麼要這樣羞辱我？」克勞狄説：「妳以為溫柔的慰藉可以讓我變得堅毅嗎？若我終究得死，我會把黑暗當作新娘，將它擁入懷裡。」

「這才像是我弟弟説的話。」伊莎貝拉説：「這才是父親墳裡傳出來的聲音。你是終究得死，但是克勞狄，你想得到嗎？那個貌似聖人的攝政説，只要我把貞操獻給他，他就饒你一命。啊，如果他要的是我的命，為了救你，我會像丟一根針一樣，毫不在乎地就給他！」

「謝謝妳，親愛的伊莎貝拉。」克勞狄説。

「你該為明天的受死做準備了。」伊莎貝拉說。

「死亡是件很恐怖的事。」克勞狄說。

「但可恥的生活令人痛恨。」他的姐姐回答。

此時，克勞狄一想到死亡，他堅定的個性就動搖了。只有臨死的罪犯才能感受到那種恐懼的侵襲，他叫道：「好姐姐，讓我活下去！妳犯罪是為了要救弟弟一命，上天會恩准這種行為，它會成為一種美德的呀。」

P.105 「哦，意志不堅的懦夫！虛偽卑鄙的小人！」伊莎貝拉說：「你要讓你姐蒙羞來苟且偷生？哦，呸，呸，呸！弟弟，我還以為你是個很有榮譽感的人，以為你要是有二十顆腦袋，寧可上二十個斷頭台，也不願讓自己的姐姐受這種屈恥。」

「不，伊莎貝拉，妳聽我說！」克勞狄說。

他想為自己辯解，解釋自己為何軟弱到要靠貞潔的姐姐屈節來苟活，但公爵走了進來，打斷他的話。

P.106 公爵說：「克勞狄，你和你姐姐說的話我都聽到了。安哲羅絕對無意染指她，他說那些話不過是想考驗她的品德。她真的是個貞潔女子，得體地拒絕了他，他高興都來不及了。他是不可能赦免你的，你就趁剩下的一點時間來祈禱，為死亡做好準備吧。」

克勞狄後悔自己剛剛的懦弱，他說：「讓我求我姐原諒我吧！我不再眷戀生命，但求一死。」克勞狄說完就退到一旁，為自己的過錯愧疚懊悔不已。

這時公爵單獨和伊莎貝拉在一起。他稱讚她守貞不渝，說道：「上帝賦與妳美貌，也賦與妳美德。」

P.107 伊莎貝拉說：「唉，安哲羅竟這樣蒙蔽了好心的公爵！等公爵回來，若我能見到他的話，一定要揭發他的治理情況。」伊莎貝拉不知道她已經在揭發她揚言要揭發的事情了。

公爵回答：「那樣做並無不妥，但就目前的情況看來，安哲羅一定會駁倒妳的控訴的，因此妳不妨聽聽我的忠告。有個不幸女子被冤枉，我想妳可以仗義幫助她，而且還可以讓妳弟弟免受厲法。妳不但不需要讓自己貞潔的身體受到玷污，而且要是缺勤的公爵回來，知道了這件事，也會非常高興的。」

伊莎貝拉表示，只要不是壞事，他要她做什麼都行。

「有德者勇，無所畏懼。」公爵說。他接著問她，是否聽過瑪莉安娜這個人，她是在海上溺斃的偉大軍人弗烈德的妹妹。

「我聽過這個人。」伊莎貝拉說：「一說到她，聽到的都是好話。」

P.108 公爵說：「她是安哲羅的未婚妻，可是她的嫁妝都在船上跟著哥哥一起沈沒了。這不幸的女子遭受的打擊是多麼沈重呀！她哥哥對她呵護備至，可是她不但失去了這位高貴有名望的哥哥，在失去財產之後，她也失去那道貌岸然的未婚夫安哲羅的愛。他妄稱發現這位高貴女子有見不得人之事（真正的原因是她沒有了嫁妝），於是拋棄她，任她哭泣流淚，也不安慰她半點。他這樣無情無義，怎麼看她都應該對他死了心，可是就像水流遇阻，反倒愈加湍急難平，瑪莉安娜仍一如當初那樣地愛著她狠心的未婚夫。」

公爵更明白地說出他的計畫，即：伊莎貝拉去找安哲羅，表面上答應半夜去找他，如他所要求的一樣。這樣一來，她就可以得到特赦的承諾。然後讓瑪莉安娜代替她赴約，讓安哲羅在黑暗中把她當成伊莎貝拉。

P.110 「好姑娘，做這件事情毋需擔憂。」假扮的修士說：「安哲羅是她的未婚夫，讓他們這樣在一起並沒有罪。」

此計讓伊莎貝拉很高興，她照修士所吩咐的去做，修士則跑去告訴瑪莉安娜此事。在這之前，他就假扮成修士去探訪過這位不幸的女子，給她宗教輔導和親切慰問，並在其間從她本人口中得知了她不幸的遭遇。她現在當他是神職人員，一下子就答應聽他的指示行事。

見完安哲羅，伊莎貝拉便去瑪莉安娜家，公爵跟她約在那裡見面。公爵說：「妳來得正好，正是時候。那位好攝政有什麼消息？」

伊莎貝拉描述她安排此事的事宜。「安哲羅有一座四面都圍有磚牆的花園。」她說：「花園的西邊是一座葡萄園，進葡萄園要通過一道門。」
P.111 她把安哲羅交給她的兩把鑰匙拿給公爵和瑪莉安娜看，說道：「這把比較大的鑰匙是用來開葡萄園的大門，從葡萄園進入花園的小門，則是用這另一把來開。我答應他半夜會去那裡找他，而他也答應一定會饒了我弟弟一命。他輕聲低語，鬼鬼祟祟，勤奮地帶我走了兩次路，我仔細謹慎地記下那個地方。」

「你們有沒有設下什麼暗號，瑪莉安娜必得遵守？」公爵問。

「沒，沒有暗號。」伊莎貝拉回答：「只說天黑時過去。我跟他說我只能待一會兒，因為我讓他相信有一個僕人會陪我來，僕人以為我是為我弟弟的事情前來。」
P.112 公爵稱讚她安排得周到。她轉向瑪莉安娜，說道：「妳不需要對安哲羅說什麼，離開他時，只需低聲細語地說：『記得我弟弟的事！』」

當天晚上，伊莎貝拉帶瑪莉安娜到約定之處。伊莎貝拉很高興，心想這個辦法既能救弟弟一命，又能保住自己的貞潔。

公爵很不放心她弟弟的性命安危，於是半夜再度造訪監獄。也幸虧他去找克勞狄，要不然克勞狄當晚就遭斬首了。因為公爵走進牢裡不久，狠心的攝政就送來一道命令，下令斬首克勞狄，並在清晨五點時把首級送到他面前。

公爵說服獄吏延緩對克勞狄行刑，而為了瞞過安哲羅，他勸他把凌晨一個命喪牢中者的人頭送去給他。
P.113 但獄吏當時認為他不過是個修士而生疑，為了說服獄吏同意，公爵就拿一封公爵的親筆信給獄吏看，上面還用公爵的封印封緘。獄吏看過之後，推想修士一定獲有缺勤公爵的秘密指令，便同意放過克勞狄，然後把那個死者的腦袋瓜砍下來，帶去給安哲羅。

之後公爵用他的真實身分寫了一封信給安哲羅，信上表示因為某些意外，他將結束旅程，隔天早上就會返抵維也納，並吩咐安哲羅在城門迎候並交還政權。公爵還命令安哲羅發出公告說，百姓凡欲控訴不公，可待他一進城門，就在街上公開申訴。

伊莎貝拉一大早來到監獄，公爵已經在那裡等她。因機密所需，公爵認為告訴她克勞狄已經被斬首較為妥當。因此當伊莎貝拉問安哲羅是否已經赦免她弟弟時，他回答：「安哲羅已經處決了克勞狄，他的頭被砍下來，送去給攝政了。」

P.114 傷心欲絕的姐姐叫喊著：「不幸的克勞狄啊，可憐的伊莎貝拉啊，害人的世界啊，好狠毒的安哲羅啊！」

假扮的修士請她節哀，待她平靜些後，他告訴她公爵即將返回，又教她該如何控告安哲羅，並表示若案情一時不利於她，也別擔心。充分指示過伊莎貝拉後，他又去找瑪莉安娜，告訴她該如何進行。

公爵脫下修士服，穿上自己的貴族長袍，效忠他的民眾簇集迎接他，他就在歡欣鼓舞的人潮中進入維也納城。安哲羅也在此迎接他，正式交回政權。

P.115 這時伊莎貝拉出現，她以申訴者的姿態投訴說：「冤枉啊！最尊貴的公爵呀！我是一個叫做克勞狄的人的姐姐，克勞狄因為誘拐一名少女，被判斬首。我請求安哲羅大人赦免我弟弟，我是怎樣下跪哀求，他是怎樣拒絕我，我又是怎樣回應他，這都說來話長，不需對您多提。我現在帶著悲痛和羞恥，要說明那可惡的結果。安哲羅要我答應他無恥的求愛，才肯放過我弟弟。我內心不斷掙扎，最後我對弟弟的憐憫勝過了我的矜持，我對他屈服了。但隔天一大清早，安哲羅就背信，下令將我不幸的弟弟斬首！」

公爵佯裝不相信她的話。安哲羅表示，她弟弟依律如法被處死後，她因為傷心而神智失常。

P.116 這時又出現了另一個投訴者：瑪莉安娜。瑪莉安娜說：「高貴的親王啊，光線來自天上，真理出自口中。真理之中有常理，道德之中有真理。仁慈的殿下啊，我是此人之妻，伊莎貝拉的話都是騙人的。她說她那晚和安哲羅在一起，事實上那晚我都和他待在花園的房子裡。我說的都是真的，請讓我平身，不然就讓我成為大理石雕像，永遠固定在這裡。」

P.117 這時伊莎貝拉請求傳喚羅德維修士，證明她所言屬實，羅德維就是公爵喬裝時所用的假名。

伊莎貝拉和瑪莉安娜所言，都是依照公爵的指示。公爵打算在全維也納人民面前公開證明伊莎貝拉的清白，安哲羅萬萬想不到，正因如此，她們兩人的供詞才會不同。安哲羅想藉由兩人供詞的矛盾，把伊莎貝拉所要控告他的罪名洗刷乾淨。他裝出一副被冤枉的無辜表情，說道：「到現在，臣都只是一笑置之，但是殿下，臣的耐心已經到達極限，臣想這兩個可憐的瘋女人不過是被利用罷了，幕後有個更大的黑手在指使她們。殿下呀，就讓臣來調查這樁陰謀吧。」

「好，我非常贊成。」公爵説：「你高興怎麼處置她們，就怎麼處置她們吧。你，艾斯卡大臣，你陪他一道審問，全力支持他去查究這宗誹謗案。我已經下令傳喚指使她們的修士了，修士來了以後，你可以依你所蒙受的損失，給他應有的懲罰。我要離開你們一會兒，但安哲羅大臣，在未完全判決好這宗誹謗案之前，你不可以離開。」

P.118 公爵説完就離開。安哲羅很滿意能夠擔任代理法官，做自己這樁案件的仲裁人。

公爵只走開了一會兒，他卸下貴族長袍，穿上修士服。喬裝之後，他又回到安哲羅和艾斯卡面前。好心的老艾斯卡以為安哲羅遭到誣告，就對喬裝的修士説：「先生，你有指使這兩位女子誹謗安哲羅大臣嗎？」

修士回答：「公爵在哪裡？應該是他來聽證的。」

艾斯卡回答：「我們就代表公爵，我們聽證，你實話實説。」

「至少我會放膽地説。」修士回嘴道。他指責公爵不該把伊莎貝拉的控訴案交給她所要控訴的人，又不諱言説他是維也納城的一個旁觀者，看到了很多腐敗的事。艾斯卡揚言，他的言論反叛政府，謫責公爵的操守，要受酷刑，打入牢裡。這時假扮的修士卸下偽裝，眾人認出是公爵本人，莫不吃驚，安哲羅尤其驚慌。

P.120 公爵先對伊莎貝拉説：「伊莎貝拉，妳過來。妳的修士現在是妳的親王了，我換了衣服，可是我的心並沒有變，仍衷心為你服務。」

「啊，請饒恕我呀。」伊莎貝拉説：「小民不知情，竟然勞煩了殿下。」

他表示，他未能制止她弟弟的死刑，才真需要她原諒——為了進一步考驗她的品德，他還不想告訴她克勞狄還活著。

安哲羅如今知曉公爵暗中親眼看到他所做的勾當，便説：「啊，威嚴的殿下呀，見到殿下本領非凡，知悉臣的行為，臣若想再掩飾，就是罪加一等。請英明的殿下莫讓臣再羞慚下去，就把臣的招供當做是問罪，只求殿下隆恩，立刻賜臣一死。」

P.121 公爵回答：「安哲羅，你罪證確鑿，我們就送你上克勞狄彎腰受刑的斷頭臺上，同樣速速行刑。至於他的財產，瑪莉安娜，我們要判給妳。名義上妳是他的寡婦，妳可以用這筆財產去找一個更好的丈夫。」

「啊，仁慈的殿下！」瑪莉安娜説：「我不要別人，也不要更好的男人。」説著她跪下來，就像伊莎貝拉求饒克勞狄一命那樣，這個賢妻為不知圖報的丈夫安哲羅求饒性命。她説：「仁慈的君王，啊，好殿下呀！好心的伊莎貝拉，幫幫我吧！跟我一起下跪求情吧，我今生終報以犬馬之勞！」

P.122 公爵説:「妳求她是很不合情理的,要是伊莎貝拉也下跪懇求開恩,她弟弟的鬼魂就要破墓而出,含恨地帶走她了。」

但瑪莉安娜仍説:「伊莎貝拉,好心的伊莎貝拉,妳只要跪在我旁邊,舉起手,不用説話,一切由我來説就行了!大家都説,至善者是由錯誤中鍛鍊而來的,大部分的人都因犯了些過失而變得更好,我的丈夫也可能如此呀。哦,伊莎貝拉,妳跟我一起下跪好嗎?」

P.123 公爵説:「他要償克勞狄一命。」

可是當伊莎貝拉也在他面前跪下時,好心的公爵心下甚喜,他始終期盼她行事仁厚正直。伊莎貝拉説:「慈恩浩蕩的君王,若殿下願意,就把這個被判死刑的人當作是我還活著的弟弟吧。在他遇見我之前,我諒他所作所為還算忠於職責。既然如此,且饒他一命吧!我弟弟只是接受法治,觸法而死。」

看到這位高貴的求情者為仇人性命説情,公爵的最佳回應就是:派人把仍以為自己命運未卜的克勞狄從牢裡帶出來,把他活生生地交給為他哀悼的伊莎貝拉。公爵對伊莎貝拉説:「伊莎貝拉,把手給我。看在妳這可愛人兒的份上,我赦免了克勞狄。若妳願意嫁給我,那他也就是我的弟弟了。」

安哲羅大臣一時之間感到自己已經安全無虞,公爵看到他眼睛隱約為之一亮,就説道:「好了,安哲羅,你可得疼愛你的夫人呀,是她的美德讓你得到赦免的。瑪莉安娜,恭喜妳了!安哲羅,好好愛她!我聽過她的告白,知道她的美德。」

P.125 安哲羅想起自己在代理職權的那段短短時間裡,是如何的鐵石心腸。如今,他才嚐到慈悲的滋味是如何甜美。

公爵命令克勞狄迎娶茱麗葉,自己則又再一次向伊莎貝拉求婚。她的美德和高貴的情操,讓她贏得親王的愛。

伊莎貝拉尚未正式成為修女,可以結婚。高貴的公爵偽裝成卑微的修士時,曾經好心地幫助過她,她於是欣然感恩地接受了他給予的光榮。伊莎貝拉成為維也納的公爵夫人後,她的高尚品德樹立了了良好典範,全城的年輕姑娘從此完全變了個樣,再也沒有人像茱麗葉那樣地越矩。而今,後悔的茱麗葉,也成為那改過自新的克勞狄之妻了。寬厚仁慈的公爵和他鍾愛的伊莎貝拉統治了好些年,他是最幸福的丈夫和親王了。